THE OLD MAID

THE OLD MAID

DOVER THRIFT EDITIONS

Edith Wharton

Introduction by
Roxana Robinson

DOVER PUBLICATIONS, INC.
MINEOLA, NEW YORK

DOVER THRIFT EDITIONS

GENERAL EDITOR: SUSAN L. RATTINER
EDITOR OF THIS VOLUME: JIM MILLER

Bibliographical Note

This Dover edition, first published in 2019, is an unabridged republication of the work originally serialized in *The Red Book Magazine* from February to April 1922. The Introduction by Roxana Robinson was first published in The Modern Library Classics edition, New York, in 2003.

Library of Congress Cataloging-in-Publication Data

Names: Wharton, Edith, 1862–1937, author. | Robinson, Roxana, author of introduction.
Title: The old maid / Edith Wharton ; introduction by Roxana Robinson.
Description: Dover edition. | Mineola, New York : Dover Publications, Inc., 2019. | Series: Dover thrift editions | "This Dover edition, first published in 2019, is an unabridged republication of the work originally serialized in The Red Book Magazine from February to April 1922. The introduction by Roxana Robinson was first published in The Modern Library Classics edition, New York, in 2003."
Identifiers: LCCN 2019008577 | ISBN 9780486836010 | ISBN 0486836010
Subjects: LCSH: Psychological fiction. | Domestic fiction.
Classification: LCC PS3545.H16 O43 2019 | DDC 813/.5—2dc23
LC record available at https://lccn.loc.gov/2019008577

Manufactured in the United States by LSC Communications
83601002   2020
www.doverpublications.com

Contents

Introduction   v

Chapter I   1

Chapter II   13

Chapter III   19

Chapter IV   23

Chapter V   31

Chapter VI   35

Chapter VII   39

Chapter VIII   43

Chapter IX   51

Chapter X   57

Chapter XI   63

INTRODUCTION

by Roxana Robinson

IN HER MEMOIR, *A Backward Glance*, Edith Wharton describes a moment in Newport of the 1870s: a group of graceful young women, gathered on a summer lawn for a meeting of the archery club. The bright sun, the green space, the sparkling sea air set off these maids, who wear white "floating silks or muslins, with their wide leghorn hats, and heavy veils flung back only at the moment of aiming."

Their faces are completely hidden. The heavy veils are wrapped around their hats, stretched over their features, tucked carefully around their necks. This was for protection, to keep the translucent skin from being raked by sunlight or roughened by sea-wind. In that world, beauty was paramount, and "No grace," wrote Wharton, "was rated as high as 'a complexion.' It is hard to picture nowadays the shell-like transparence, the luminous red-and-white of those young cheeks untouched by paint and powder, in which the blood came and went like the lights of an aurora. Beauty was unthinkable without 'a complexion,' and to defend that treasure against sun and wind . . . veils as thick as curtains . . . were habitually worn. It must have been very uncomfortable to the wearers, who could hardly see or breathe: but even to my childish eyes the effect was dazzling when the curtain was drawn, and young beauty shone forth."

Striking as is this image of transparency and beauty, even more so is the notion of cherishing and protection implied by the closely veiled faces: these young women were jewels. Their loveliness—source of their attraction, sign of their worth—was carefully guarded. Their luminous, glowing skin was masked against the burning sunlight, their lissome forms were blurred by floating silks, even their own vision was obscured by close-woven shields. Exposure meant risk. Chaperoned, attended, they lived under close familial scrutiny during the perilous age of marriageability, revealed only, briefly, during "the moment of aiming." When the shaft had struck its mark, the bridegroom stepped forward with the proprietary right to lift the veil. Until then, these closely swathed and virginal figures, emblems of value and virtue in Wharton's "Old New York," led a chaste and cloistered life. They were governed by strict social codes, obedient to fixed and immutable laws.

And yet . . . and yet. Is it ever possible to live according to fixed and immutable laws? Were there moments in which those veils were privately loosened, secretly lifted?

★   ★   ★

Edith Jones Wharton was born in 1862 into the fashionable inner circles of New York, a fact that would reverberate throughout her fiction. Providing both setting and drama, the world of the well-bred was portrayed in endless variations within her work. This was a small, tribal society with a strict caste system, governed by copious and inflexible laws. These addressed every sort of comportment, from the paying of social calls to the arbitration of morality. Obedience to them was a requisite for membership in the community; breaking them meant the risk of expulsion.

Edith Wharton obeyed the rules. She married a young man of good family, joined the "young married set" in New York, and spent summers in Newport. Her life, however, was one of increasing isolation, both emotional and intellectual: her husband was unfaithful and unstable, and her circles excluded writers. After twenty-eight years of marriage, Wharton broke the rules, divorcing her husband. In 1913 she moved to France, where she spent the rest of her life. Paris, more tolerant and sophisticated than New York, welcomed her into the rich, vital mix of the salon—despite her being female, intellectual, and divorced.

Though Wharton had left old New York, it was deeply engrained within her. She had broken its rules but she respected their potency. Her perceptions of this world would change, but it would remain at the center of her experience, and it would be central to her best work.

In 1905, still married, still in New York, Wharton published *The House of Mirth*. In this elegant tragedy, beautiful, impecunious Lily Bart is unable to survive within the heartless and superficial world of New York Society. Though we Lily, we cannot imagine her happiness in this deadly, vapid place, with its rigid rules, idle pastimes, and disloyal, adulterous friends. The social code here seems punitive and empty—form without substance.

The Custom of the Country (1913) addressed the subversive issue of divorce—fresh in Wharton's mind. The shrewd adventuress Undine Spragg trades her troth repeatedly for advancement. Deftly she climbs the social ladder, grasping, with the aid of accommodating husbands, at ever higher prizes. The old world here is elegant, faded, and moribund, its laws powerless over someone so vulgar and materialistic, who values neither tradition nor family. The new world, that of the arriviste, is worse: glittering, cold, and dreadful.

At the end of World War I, Wharton, in her late fifties, was deeply affected by the grief that blanketed her adopted country. The brilliant world she had loved had vanished; she felt *dipaysée*. She told a friend sadly, "*Fe me cherche, et je ne me trouue pas.*" Nineteenth-century America was gone; twentieth-century America was alien. "All that I thought American in a true sense is gone, and I see nothing but vain-glory, crassness and a total ignorance . . . ," she wrote. She began to reconsider the old, lost world. What had seemed once petty and insular now seemed valuable and dignified; the rules, she saw, had been founded on moral principle. "I am steeping myself in the nineteenth century," she wrote, ". . . such a blessed refuge from the turmoil and mediocrity of today—like taking sanctuary in a mighty temple."

In 1919–1920, Wharton wrote *The Age of Innocence*, set in the 1870s. This exquisite, elegiac work, with its themes of love and renunciation, is her most powerful tribute to that lost world. Here the strict social codes are part of a larger moral imperative, one that protects the community at the expense of the individual. Ellen Olenska and Newland Archer sacrifice their own happiness for that of others, nobly upholding an ideal of honor and the greater good.

In 1921, still mining the rich vein of the past, Wharton began a quartet of novellas, tilted collectively *Old New York*. Each dealt with a nineteenth-century decade: *False Dawn: The 'Forties; The Old Maid: The 'Fifties; The Spark: The 'Sixties;* and *New Years Day: The 'Seventies*. Published in separate volumes, in 1924, they were declared by *The New York Times* to be among Wharton's best work. *The Old Maid* was called "one of the most beautiful stories in the whole range of American literature." It sold three times as well as the others, though periodicals had rejected it as "too unpleasant."

The Old Maid, written in 1921, is indeed beautiful in its construction, and its subject is indeed unpleasant. Like Wharton's bleak tale of retribution, *Ethan Frome*, this delivers truths we might rather not know. *The Old Maid*, however, is more complex and more assured than the earlier work. The execution is brilliant and the construction nearly flawless: Wharton weaves a golden, fine-meshed net about her characters with inexorable precision.

The Old Maid is set in a staid, unimaginative society, embodied by the stolid and conventional Ralston family, "of middle-class English stock." They are industrious, decent, and deeply cautious; heroism is seen as too risky. Their sensibility provides the moral backdrop to the story.

The narrative centers on two women. As in much of Wharton's fiction, the men play minor roles. Few male characters in her work—or her life—were both powerful and principled, and here the men are largely passive or absent. The protagonists are Delia and Charlotte, Lovell cousins. Delia, the beauty, from a comfortable background, has married steady Jim Ralston. She has two pretty children and a pretty bedroom in a pretty house on Gramercy Park. She is happy being a Ralston, though she remembers the man she did not marry: impetuous Clement Spender, who chose art in Rome over law in New York.

Charlotte, by contrast, is a poor Lovell, and plain, with eyes and hair a pale common brown. Her father died young, and her widowed mother was unable to help her enter Society. Charlotte languished in the marriage-market, then tuberculosis flushed her cheek with its sinister stain. But now Charlotte is healthy again, and engaged to Joe Ralston. Her face is nearly pretty; even her hair seems darker. She has sailed into safe harbor.

The scene is set for complications: Delia admires herself in her mirror as Charlotte arrives, distraught, and throws herself on Delia's love seat. The complications unfold like the petals of an intricate flower. Issues emerge: secrecy, the violation of codes. Betrayal. Deception. Jealousy, compassion, rage. Retribution, love. The unthinkable: sexuality.

In her photographs, Edith Wharton is so straight-backed, so correct. Her hair is so impeccably smooth, her wide pearl choker so high and tight. Her demeanor shows such formality and restraint. And her writing is as elegant and formal as her demeanor: how can this decorous person have such thoughts? How can these polished, mannerly sentences describe such improprieties? But they do: Wharton's work is full of the wide dark tide of sexuality, its roiling luxuriance, its sweet potency.

Like all novelists, Wharton drew on her own experience, and there are parallels between her own mother, Lucretia, and that of Charlotte. Lucretia was "a poor Rhinelander" whose widowed mother gave her little help. Both women wore hand-me-down slippers to their coming-out balls; both had grandmothers with yellow coaches and fringed hammer-cloths. But there the stories diverged: Lucretia married a man of good family, put poverty behind her, and led a decorous, conventional life. Or did they diverge completely? Was there a connecting thread? A scarlet one?

Edith's birth—the last in the family—must have been something of a surprise: there were twelve long years between herself and her closest brother. It was widely rumored that the reason for this was Edith's paternity—that her father was not Frederic Jones, but the young English tutor living with the family, teaching Edith's brothers. Edith was said to resemble the young man to a shocking degree. R.W. B. Lewis, Wharton's biographer, thinks the rumors were unfounded, but what is known to be true is that Edith was aware of them. She understood that such a thing could happen in her small, strictly controlled world—even in her family's small, strictly controlled household. She knew the unthinkable was possible.

Sexual knowledge is the fulcrum on which *The Old Maid* turns, as its name suggests. The knowledge was charged, forbidden, secret. The young women of this era were to arrive at the altar virginal and untouched, unsullied even by information. The chaste Delia, on her wedding night, was mystified but obedient, yielding to her husband's incomprehensible demands.

Charlotte's sexual initiation was different. Poor and plain, she did not attract the attentions of the man she loved. Without attentive parents, she lacked guardianship; unchaperoned, she yielded to the importunate advances of a man she loves but who, she knows, does not love her, and, worse, will not marry her. The illicit scene is thrillingly imagined by Delia: the dark parlor, the swathed chandelier; the infirm grandmother and servants asleep on the upper floors; the silent lovers in the moonlight. It is a scene infinitely more urgent and compelling than Delia's modest, confused initiation in the big white bed. Because of this secret passage, poor plain Charlotte is suddenly revealed as more exotic, more dangerous and glamorous; more worldly and knowing than the matronly, domestic Delia.

There is no greater social crime, no greater transgression of the codes, than for a girl of good breeding to have an illegitimate child. The laws are implacable; retribution inescapable. Charlotte must be

punished for her illicit knowledge, and the instrument of the law, its
enforcer, is her chaste and decorous cousin. It is Delia who upholds
the code of the Ralstons, who undertakes to protect the community—and not simply on moral grounds. Her attitude is marvelously
complicated, for Delia's thick braid of righteousness contains not
only a bright strand of compassion—for wouldn't it be possible
somehow to salvage Charlotte's happiness?—but also a vivid strand
of envy. Hasn't her poorer, plainer cousin taken something that Delia
believed was hers? The lover, Delia learns, is Clement Spender, and
didn't he belong to her? This secret sense of betrayal turns Delia
high-handed, imperious, and relentless. Her personal outrage feeds
her moral and, like an avenging deity, Delia the Chaste metes out
Charlotte's punishment.

There are connections between *The Old Maid* and *The Age of
Innocence*. Ellen was originally named Clementina Olenska. The two
lovers—Ellen and Newland—were to consummate their love, before
parting forever. But the most significant connection lies in the func-
tioning of the moral code. In both stories, the laws of the community
must be served absolutely, protecting the institutions—marriage, the
family, the legitimacy of bloodline—at great and painful cost to the
individual.

Charlotte must be punished for her knowledge, and Delia
rewarded for her chastity. Charlotte relinquishes all public maternal
rights and privileges in exchange for remaining within the community. Her persona is transmuted the beloved one of the Virgin—
rich with the possibilities of the future—to the despised one of the
Old Maid—symbol of emotiomal and biological barrenness. The
law-abiding Delia is given infinite power over her sinful cousin.
Both of them adore Charlotte's beautiful child, Tina, who has a
charged fascination for them. Tina represents the life each woman
might have had, and for which each secretly yearns. As the story's
knots twist tighter and tighter, the issue of illicit sexual knowledge arises again, this time over the risk to Tina. Charlotte, fiercely
protective, prepares boldly to leave the community, taking Tina
elsewhere to seek a legitimate, more modest life. Delia, desperate
to keep Tina, exquisitely cruel, accuses Charlotte of sacrificing her
daughter to her own "desire for mastery."

Each woman loves the child; each wants to claim motherhood.
Each uses the other for the child's good. But power lies with Delia
the Chaste, and with each excruciating turn of the plot, Charlotte
loses more of her maternal connection. With each new binding

twist, Wharton imposes the lessons of this forbidden knowledge, the iron inexorability of the law that governs it.

Charlotte's sacrifice has, however, achieved its goal; these laws are strict but just. Charlotte has given up a mother's role to become an object of charity, sacrificing her life for her daughter's future. But she has remained within the community, and Tina has been accepted. The child has been cherished, given a name and a dowry. On the eve of her wedding (to a young man of good family) Tina is legitimate, modestly affluent—and still innocent.

In the final conflict, the rival mothers clash over Tina's prenuptial instruction. The old issues emerge: Charlotte's deep and endless wound, Delia's struggle between envy and compassion. Charlotte yields; then Delia foregoes the privilege. The bride will still remain innocent, unaware of sexual knowledge or its cost. The struggle is over: Charlotte has yielded the last scrap of motherhood to Delia. The law has been obeyed, the price paid, and the punishment is complete.

Delia the Chaste, the avenger, satisfied by Charlotte's expiation, now relents. Revealing her compassionate aspect, Delia bestows a final blessing on both mother and daughter—now that she has, victorious, separated them forever.

★ ★ ★

ROXANA ROBINSON is the author of two previous novels, a biography of Georgia O'Keeffe, and two short-story collections. She has received fellowships from the Guggenheim Foundation, the National Endowment for the Arts, and the MacDowell Colony. Robinson's fiction has appeared in *Best American Short Stories, The Atlantic, The New Yorker, Harper's,* and *Vogue*. She lives in New York City and Westchester County, New York.

THE OLD MAID

CHAPTER I

IN THE OLD New York of the 'thirties a few families ruled, in simplicity and affluence. Of these were the Ralstons. The sturdy English and the rubicund and heavier Dutch had mingled to produce a prosperous, prudent and yet lavish society. To "do things handsomely" had always been a fundamental principle in this cautious world, built up on the fortunes of bankers, India merchants, shipbuilders, and shipchandlers. Those well-fed, slow-moving people, who seemed irritable and dyspeptic to European eyes only because the caprices of the climate had stripped them of superfluous flesh, and strung their nerves a little tighter, lived in a genteel monotony of which the surface was never stirred by the dumb dramas now and then enacted underground. Sensitive souls in those days were like muted keyboards, on which Fate played without a sound.

In this compact society, built of solidly welded blocks, one of the largest areas was filled by the Ralstons and their ramifications. The Ralstons were of middle-class English stock. They had not come to the colonies to die for a creed but to live for a bank-account. The result had been beyond their hopes, and their religion was tinged by their success. An edulcorated Church of England which, under the conciliatory name of the "Episcopal Church of the United States of America," left out the coarser allusions in the Marriage Service, slid over the comminatory passages in the Athanasian Creed, and thought it more respectful to say "Our Father *who*" than "*which*" in the Lord's Prayer, was exactly suited to the spirit of compromise whereon the Ralstons had built themselves up. There was in all the tribe the same instinctive recoil from new religions as from unaccounted-for people. Institutional to the core, they represented the conservative element that holds new societies together as seaplants bind the seashore.

1

Compared with the Ralstons, even such traditionalists as the Lovells, the Halseys or the Vandergraves appeared careless, indifferent to money, almost reckless in their impulses and indecisions. Old John Frederick Ralston, the stout founder of the race, had perceived the difference, and emphasized it to his son, Frederick John, in whom he had scented a faint leaning toward the untried and unprofitable.

"You let the Lannings and the Dagonets and the Spenders take risks and fly kites. It's the county-family blood in 'em: we've nothing to do with that. Look how they're petering out already—the men, I mean. Let your boys marry their girls, if you like (they're wholesome and handsome); though I'd sooner see my grandsons take a Lovell or a Vandergrave, than any of our own kind. But don't let your sons go mooning around with their young fellows, horseracing, and running down south to those damned springs, and gambling at New Orleans, and all the rest of it. That's how you'll build up the family, and keep the weather out. The way we've always done it."

Frederick John listened, obeyed, married a Halsey, and passively followed in his father's steps. He belonged to the cautious generation of New York gentlemen who revered Hamilton and served Jefferson, who longed to lay out New York like Washington, and who laid it out instead like a gridiron, lest they should be thought "undemocratic" by people they secretly looked down upon. Shopkeepers to the marrow, they put in their windows the wares there was most demand for, keeping their private opinions for the back-shop, where, through lack of use, they gradually lost substance and color.

The present generation of Ralstons had nothing left in the way of convictions save an acute sense of honor in private and business matters; on the life of the community and the state they took their daily views from the newspapers, and the newspapers they already despised. They themselves had done little to shape the destiny of their country, except to finance the Cause when it had become safe to do so. They were related to many of the great men who had built the Republic; but no Ralston had so far committed himself as to be great. As old John Frederick said, it was safer to be satisfied with three per cent: they regarded heroism as a form of gambling. Yet by merely being so numerous and so similar they had come to have a weight in the community. People said, "The Ralstons," when they wished to invoke a precedent. This attribution of authority had gradually convinced the third generation of its collective importance; and the fourth, to which Delia Ralston's husband belonged, had the ease and simplicity of a ruling class.

Within the limits of their universal caution, the Ralstons fulfilled their obligations as rich and respected citizens. They figured on the boards of all the old-established charities, gave handsomely to thriving institutions, had the best cooks in New York, and when they traveled abroad ordered statuary of the American sculptors in Rome whose reputation was already made. The first Ralston who had brought home a statue had been regarded as a wild fellow; but when it became known that the sculptor had executed several orders for the British aristocracy, it was felt in the family that this too was a three-per-cent investment.

Two marriages with the Dutch Vandergraves had consolidated these qualities of thrift and handsome living, and the carefully built-up Ralston character was now so congenital that Delia Ralston sometimes asked herself whether, were she to turn her little boy loose in a wilderness, he would not create a small New York there, and be on all its boards of directors.

Delia Lovell had married James Ralston at twenty. The marriage, which had taken place in the month of September, 1840, had been solemnized, as was then the custom, in the drawing-room of the bride's country home, at what is now the corner of Avenue A and Ninety-first Street, overlooking the Sound. Thence her husband had driven her (in Grandmamma Lovell's canary-colored coach with a fringed hammer-cloth), through spreading suburbs and untidy elm-shaded streets, to one of the new houses in Gramercy Park, which the pioneers of the younger set were just beginning to affect; and there, at five-and-twenty, she was established, the mother of two children, the possessor of a generous allowance of pin-money, and, by common consent, one of the handsomest and most popular "young matrons" (as they were called) of her day.

She was thinking placidly and gratefully of these things as she sat one day in her handsome bedroom in Gramercy Park. She was too near to the primitive Ralstons to have as clear a view of them as, for instance, the son in question might one day command: she lived under them as unthinkingly as one lives under the laws of one's country. Yet that tremor in her of the muted keyboard, that secret questioning which sometimes beat in her like wings, would now and then so divide her from them that for a fleeting moment she could survey them in their relation to other things. The moment was always fleeting: she dropped back from it quickly, breathless and a little pale, to her children, her housekeeping, her new dresses and her kindly Jim.

She thought of him today with a smile of tenderness, remembering how he had told her to spare no expense on her new bonnet. Though she was twenty-five, and twice a mother, her image was still surprisingly fresh. The plumpness then thought seemly in a young matron stretched the gray silk across her bosom, and caused her heavy gold watch-chain—after it left the anchorage of the brooch of St. Peter's in mosaic that fastened her low-cut Cluny collar—to dangle perilously in the void, above a tiny waist buckled into a velvet waist-band. But the shoulders above sloped youthfully under her Cashmere scarf, and every movement was as quick as a girl's.

*   *   *

Mrs. Ralston approvingly examined the rosy-cheeked oval set in the blonde ruffles of the bonnet on which, in compliance with her husband's instructions, she had spared no expense. It was a cabriolet of white velvet tied with wide satin ribbons and plumed with a crystal-spangled marabou—a wedding bonnet ordered for the marriage of her cousin, Charlotte Lovell, which was to take place that week at St. Mark's-in-the-Bouwerie. Charlotte was making a match exactly like Delia's own: marrying a Ralston, of the Waverley Place branch, than which nothing could be safer, sounder or more—well, usual. Delia did not know why the word had occurred to her, for it could hardly be postulated, even of the young women of her own narrow clan, that they "usually" married Ralstons; but the soundness, safeness, suitability of the arrangement, did make it typical of the kind of alliance which a nice girl in the nicest set would serenely and blushfully forecast for herself.

Yes—and afterward?

Well—what? And what did this new question mean? Afterward; why, of course, there was the startled, unprepared surrender to the incomprehensible exigencies of the man to whom one had at most accorded a rosy cheek in return for an engagement ring; there was the large double bed; the terror of seeing him shaving calmly the next morning, in his shirt-sleeves, through the dressing-room door; the evasions, insinuations, resigned smiles and Bible texts of one's Mamma; the reminder of the phrase "to obey" in the glittering blur of the Marriage Service: a week or a month of flushed distress, confusion, embarrassed pleasure; then the growth of habit, the insidious lulling of the matter-of-course, dreamless double slumbers in the big white bed, early-morning discussions and consultations through that dressing-room door which had once seemed to open into a fiery pit scorching the brow of innocence.

And then, the babies: the babies who were supposed to "make up for everything," and didn't—though they were such darlings, and one had no definite notion as to what it was that one had missed, and that they were to make up for.

Yes: Charlotte's fate would be just like hers. Joe Ralston was so like his second cousin Jim (Delia's James), that Delia could see no reason why life in the squat brick house in Waverley Place should not exactly resemble life in the tall brownstone house in Gramercy Park. Only Charlotte's bedroom would certainly not be as pretty as hers.

★   ★   ★

She glanced complacently at the French wall-paper that reproduced a watered silk, with a "valanced" border and tassels between the loops. The mahogany bedstead, covered with a white embroidered counterpane, was symmetrically reflected in the mirror of the wardrobe that matched it. Colored lithographs of the "Four Seasons" by Leopold Robert surmounted groups of family daguerruotypes in deeply recessed gilt frames. The ormolu clock represented a shepherdess sitting on a fallen trunk, a basket of flowers at her feet. A shepherd, stealing up, surprised her with a kiss, while her little dog barked at him from a clump of roses. One knew the profession of the lovers by their crooks and the shape of their hats. This frivolous timepiece had been a wedding-gift from Delia's aunt, Mrs. Manson Mingott, a dashing widow who lived in Paris and was received at the Tuileries. It had been intrusted by her to young Clement Spender, who had come back from Italy for a short holiday just after Delia's marriage: the marriage which might never have been, if Clem Spender could have supported a wife, or had consented to give up painting and Rome for New York and the law. The young man (who looked, already, so odd and foreign and sarcastic) had laughingly assured the bride that her aunt's gift was "the newest thing in the Palais Royal;" and the family, who admired Mrs. Manson Mingott's taste, though they disapproved of her "foreignness," had criticized Delia's putting the clock in her bedroom instead of displaying it on the drawing-room mantel. But she liked, when she woke in the morning, to see the bold shepherd stealing his kiss.

Charlotte would certainly not have such a pretty clock in her bedroom; but then, she had not been used to pretty things. Her father, who had died at thirty of lung-fever, was one of the "poor Lovells." His widow, burdened with a young family, and living all the year round "up the River," could not do much for her eldest girl; and Charlotte had entered society in her mother's turned garments, and shod with satin sandals handed down from a defunct great-aunt who had "opened a ball" with General Washington. The old-fashioned Ralston furniture, which Delia already saw herself gradually banishing, would seem sumptuous to Chatty; very likely she would think Delia's gay French timepiece somewhat frivolous, or even "not quite nice." Poor Charlotte had become so serious, so prudish almost, since she had given up balls and taken to visiting the poor! Delia remembered, with ever-recurring wonder, the abrupt change in her: the precise moment at which it had been privately agreed in the family that, after all, Charlotte Lovell was going to be an old maid.

They had not thought so when she came out. Though her mother could not afford to give her more than one new tarlatan dress, and though nearly everything in her appearance was regrettable, from the too bright red of her hair to the too pale brown of her eyes,—not to mention the rounds of brick-rose on her cheekbones, which almost (preposterous thought!) made her look as if she painted,—yet these defects were redeemed by a slim waist, a light foot and a gay laugh; and when her hair was well oiled and brushed for an evening party, so that it looked almost brown, and lay smoothly along her delicate cheeks, under a wreath of red and white camellias, several eligible men (Joe Ralston among them) were known to have called her pretty.

*   *   *

Then came her illness. She caught cold on a moonlight sleighing party; the brick-rose circles deepened, and she began to cough. There was a report that she was "going like her father," and she was hurried off to a remote village in Georgia, where she lived alone for a year with an old family governess. When she came back, every one felt at once that there was a change in her. She was pale, and thinner than ever, but with an exquisitely transparent cheek, darker eyes and redder hair; and the oddness of her appearance was increased by plain dresses of Quakerish cut. She had left off trinkets and watch-chains, always wore the same gray cloak and small close bonnet, and displayed a sudden zeal for visiting the poor. The family explained that during her year in the South she had been shocked by the hopeless degradation of the "poor whites" and their children, and that this revelation of misery had made it impossible for her to return to the light-hearted life of her contemporaries. Everyone agreed, with an exchange of significant glances, that this unnatural state of mind would "pass off in time;" and meanwhile old Mrs. Lovell, Chatty's grandmother, who understood her perhaps better than the others, gave her a little money for her paupers, and lent her a room in the Lovell stables (at the back of the old Mercer Street house) where she gathered about her, in what would afterward have been called a "day-nursery," some of the poor children of the neighborhood.

There was even, among them, the baby girl whose origin had excited such intense curiosity in the neighborhood two or three years earlier, when a veiled lady in handsome clothes had brought it to the hovel of Cyrus Washington, the negro handy-man whose wife Jessamine took in Dr. Lanskell's washing. Dr. Lanskell was the chief practitioner of the day, and presumably versed in the secret history of every household from the Battery to Union Square; but though beset by inquisitive patients, he had invariably declared himself unable to identify Jessamine's "veiled lady," or to hazard a guess as to the origin of the hundred-dollar bill pinned to the baby's cloak.

The hundred dollars were never renewed; the lady never reappeared; but the baby lived healthily and happily with Jessamine's pickaninnies, and as soon as it could toddle, was brought to Chatty Lovell's day nursery, where it appeared (like its fellow-paupers) in little garments cut down from her old dresses, and socks knitted by her untiring hands. Delia, absorbed in her own babies, had nevertheless dropped in once or twice at the nursery, and had come away wishing that Chatty's maternal instinct might find its normal outlet in marriage and motherhood. The married cousin confusedly felt that her own affection for her handsome children was a mild and measured sentiment compared with Chatty's fierce passion for the plebeian waifs in Grandmamma Lovell's stable.

And then, to the general surprise, Charlotte Lovell engaged herself to Joe Ralston. It was known that had "admired her" the year she came out. She was a graceful dancer, and Joe, who was tall and nimble, had footed it with her many a reel and Schottisch. By the end of the winter all the match-makers were predicting that something would come of it; but when Delia playfully sounded her cousin, the girl's evasive answer and burning brow seemed to imply that her suitor had changed his mind, and no more questions had been asked. Now it became evident that there had, in fact, been an old romance, probably followed by that exciting incident, a "misunderstanding;" but at last all was well, and the bells of St. Mark's were about to ring in happier days for Charlotte. "Ah, when she has her first baby," the Ralston mothers chorused.

★ ★ ★

"Chatty!" Delia exclaimed, pushing back her chair as she saw her cousin's image reflected in the glass over her shoulder.

Charlotte Lovell had paused in the doorway. "They told me you were here—so I ran up."

"Of course, darling. How handsome you do look in your poplin! I always said you needed rich materials. I'm so thankful to see you out of brown cashmere."

Delia lifted her hands, and raising the white bonnet from her dark polished head, shook it so that the crystals glittered.

"I hope you like it? It's for your wedding." she laughed.

Charlotte Lovell stood motionless. In her mother's old dove-colored poplin, freshly banded with rows of crimson velvet ribbon, an ermine tippet crossed on her bosom, and a new beaver bonnet with a falling feather, she had already something of the assurance and majesty of a married woman.

"And you know your hair *is* darker, darling." Delia added, still hopefully surveying her.

"Darker? It's gray," Charlotte broke out in her deep voice, pushing back one of the pomaded bands that framed her face, and showing a white lock on her temple. "You needn't save up your bonnet. I'm not going to be married," she added harshly, with a smile that showed her teeth in a fleeting glare.

Delia had just enough presence of mind to lay down the white bonnet, marabou up, before she flung herself on her cousin.

"Not going to be married? Charlotte, are you perfectly crazy?"

"Why is it crazy to do what I think right?"

"But people said you were going to marry him the year you came out. And no one understood what happened then. And now—how can it possibly be right? You simply *can't!*" Delia incoherently summed up.

"Oh—people!" said Charlotte wearily.

Her married cousin looked at her with a start. Something thrilled in her voice that Delia had never heard in it, or in any other human voice, before. Its echo seemed to set their familiar world rocking, and the Axminster carpet actually heaved under Delia's shrinking slippers.

★ ★ ★

Charlotte stood staring ahead of her with strained lids. In the pale brown of her eyes Delia noticed the green specks that floated there when she was angry or excited.

"Charlotte—where on earth have you come from?" she cried, drawing the girl down to the sofa.

"Come from?"

"Yes. You look as if you'd seen a ghost—an army of ghosts."

The same snarling smile drew up Charlotte's lip. "I've seen Joe," she said.

"Well? . . . Oh, Chatty." Delia cried, abruptly illuminated, "you don't mean to say that you're going to let any little thing in Joe's past—not that I've ever heard the least hint, never. But if there were—" She drew a deep breath, and bravely proceeded to extremities. "Even if you've heard that he's been—that he's had a child—of course he would have provided for it before—"

The girl shook her head. "I know; you needn't go on. 'Men will be men;' but it's not that."

"Tell me what it is."

Charlotte Lovell looked about the sunny, prosperous room as if it were the image of her world, and that world were a prison she must break out of. She lowered her head. "I want—to get away," she panted.

"Get away? From Joe?"

"From his ideas—the Ralston ideas."

Delia bridled—after all, she was a Ralston! "The Ralston ideas? I haven't found them—so unbearably unpleasant to live with," she smiled a little tartly.

"No. But it was different with you: they didn't ask you to give up things."

"What things?" What in the world, Delia wondered, had poor Charlotte, that anyone could want her to give up? She had always been in the position of taking rather than of having to surrender. "Can't you explain to me, dear?" Delia urged.

"My poor children—he says I'm to give them up," cried the girl in a stricken whisper.

"Give them up? Give up helping them?"

"Seeing them—looking after them. Give them up altogether. He got his mother to explain to me. After—after we have children, he's afraid—afraid our children might catch things . . . He'll give me money, of course, to pay some one—a hired person to look after them. He thought that handsome," Charlotte broke out in a sob. She flung off her bonnet and smothered her weeping in the cushions.

* * *

Delia sat perplexed. Of all unforeseen complications this was surely the least imaginable. And with all the acquired Ralston that was in her she could not help seeing the force of Joe's objection, could almost find herself agreeing with him. No one in New York had forgotten the death of the poor Henry van der Luydens' only child, from small-pox caught at the circus to which an unprincipled nurse had surreptitiously taken him. After that warning, parents felt justified in every precaution against contagion. And poor people were so ignorant and careless, and their children, of course, so perpetually exposed to everything catching. No, Joe Ralston was certainly right, and Charlotte almost insanely unreasonable. But it would be useless to tell her so now. Instinctively, Delia temporized.

"After all," she whispered to the prone ear, "if it's only after you have children—you may not have any—for some time."

"Oh, yes, I shall!" came back in anguish from the cushions.

Delia smiled with matronly superiority. "Really, Chatty, I don't quite see how you can know. You don't understand."

Charlotte Lovell lifted herself up. Her collar of Brussels lace hung in a crumpled wisp on the loose folds of her bodice, and through the disorder of her hair the white lock glimmered haggardly. In the pale brown of her eyes the little green specks floated like leaves in a trout-pool.

"Poor girl," Delia thought, "how old and ugly she looks! More than ever like an old maid; and she seems to have no idea that she'll never have another chance."

"You must try to be sensible, Chatty dear. After all, one's own babies have the first claim."

"That's just it." The girl seized her fiercely by the wrists. "How can I give up my own baby?"

"Your—your?" Delia's world again began to waver under her. "Which of the poor little waifs, dearest, do you call your own baby?" she questioned patiently.

Charlotte looked her straight in the eyes. "I call my own baby my own baby."

"Your own—? You're hurting my wrists, Chatty." Delia freed herself, forcing a smile. "Your own—?"

"My own little girl: the one that Jessamine and Cyrus—"

"Oh—" Delia Ralston gasped.

The two cousins sat silent, facing each other; but Delia looked away. It came over her with a shudder of repugnance that such things should not have been spoken in her bedroom, so near the spotless nursery across the passage. Mechanically she smoothed the folds of her silk skirt, which her cousin's embrace had crumpled. Then she looked again at Charlotte's eyes, and her own melted.

"Oh, poor Chatty—poor Chatty!" She held out her arms to her cousin.

CHAPTER II

THE SHEPHERD continued to steal his kiss from the shepherdess, and the clock in the fallen trunk continued to tick out the minutes.

Delia, petrified, sat unconscious of their passing, her cousin clasped to her. She was dumb with the horror and amazement of learning that her own blood ran in the veins of the anonymous foundling, the "hundred-dollar baby" about whom New York had so long furtively jested and conjectured. It was her first contact with the nether side of the smooth social surface, and she sickened at the thought that such things were, and that she, Delia Ralston, should be hearing of them in her own house, from the lips of the victim! For Chatty of course was a victim—but whose? She had spoken no name, and Delia could put no question: the horror of it sealed her lips. Her mind had instantly raced back over Chatty's past; but she saw no masculine figure in it but Joe Ralston's. And to connect Joe with the episode was obviously unthinkable. Some one in the South, then? But no: Charlotte had been ill when she left—and in a flash Delia understood the real nature of that illness, and of the girl's disappearance. But from such speculations, too, her mind recoiled, and instinctively she fastened on something she could still grasp: Joe Ralston's attitude about Chatty's paupers. Of course Joe could not let his wife risk bringing home contagion—that was safe ground to dwell on. Her own Jim would have felt in the same way; and she would certainly have agreed with him.

Her eyes traveled back to the clock. She always thought of Clem Spender when she looked at the clock, and suddenly she wondered—if things had been different—what *he* would have said if she had made such an appeal to him as Charlotte had made to Joe. The thing seemed inconceivable; yet in a flash of mental readjustment she saw herself as his wife, she saw her children as his; she pictured herself asking him to let her go on caring for the poor waifs in the

13

Mercer Street stable, and she distinctly heard his laugh and his light answer: "Why on earth did you ask, you little goose? Do you take me for such a Pharisee as that?"

Yes, that was Clem Spender all over—tolerant, reckless, indifferent to consequences, always doing the kind thing at the moment, and too often leaving others to pay the score. "There's something cheap about Clem," Jim had once said in his heavy way. Delia Ralston roused herself and pressed her cousin closer. "Chatty, tell me," she whispered.

"There's nothing more."

"I mean, about yourself—this thing—this—" Clem Spender's voice was still in her ears. "You loved some one," she breathed.

"Yes. That's over . . . Now it's only the child. . . . And I could love Joe—in another way." Chatty Lovell straightened herself, wan and frowning.

"I need the money—I must have it for my baby, or else they'll send it to an institution." She paused. "But that's not all. I want to marry—to be a wife, like all of you. I should have loved Joe's children—our children. Life doesn't stop."

"No: I suppose not. But you speak as if—as if—the person who took advantage of you—"

"No one took advantage of me. I was lonely and unhappy. I met some one who was lonely and unhappy. People don't all have your luck. We were both too poor to marry each other—and Mother would never have consented. And so one day—one day before he said good-by—"

"He said good-by?"

"Yes. He was going to leave the country."

"To leave the country—knowing? "

"How was he to know? He doesn't live here. He'd just come back—come back to see his family—for a few weeks—" She broke off, her thin lips pressed together upon her secret.

* * *

There was a silence. Delia stared at the bold shepherd.

"Come back from where?" she suddenly asked in a low tone.

"Oh, what does it matter? You wouldn't understand." Charlotte broke off irritably, in the very words her married cousin had com-passionately addressed to her virginity.

A slow blush rose to Delia's cheek: she felt oddly humiliated by the rebuke conveyed in that contemptuous retort. She seemed to herself shy, ineffectual, as incapable as an ignorant girl of dealing with the abominations that Charlotte was thrusting on her. But suddenly some fierce feminine intuition struggled and woke in her. She forced her eyes upon her cousin's.

"You won't tell me who it was?"

"What's the use? I haven't told anybody."

"Then why have you come to me?"

Charlotte's stony face broke up in weeping. "It's for my baby— my baby—"

Delia did not heed her. "How can I help you if I don't know?" she insisted in a harsh, dry voice: her heartbeats were so violent that they felt like a throttling hand at her throat.

Charlotte made no answer.

"Come back from where?" Delia doggedly repeated; and at that, with a long wail, the girl flung her hands up, screening her eyes. "He always thought you'd wait for him," she sobbed out, "and then, when he found you hadn't—and that you were marrying Jim—He heard it just as he was sailing. . . . He didn't know it till Mrs. Mingott asked him to bring the clock for your wedding—"

"Stop—stop," Delia cried, springing to her feet. She had provoked the avowal, and now that it had come, she felt that it had been gratuitously and indecently thrust upon her. Was this New York, *her* New York, her safe, friendly, hypocritical New York, was this James Ralston's house, and this his wife listening to such revelations of dishonor?

★   ★   ★

Charlotte stood up in her turn. "I knew it—I knew it! You think worse of my baby now, instead of better. . . . Oh, why did you make me tell you? I knew you'd never understand. I'd always cared for him, ever since I came out; that was why I wouldn't marry anyone else. But I knew there was no hope for me—he never looked at anybody but you. And then, when he came back four years ago, and there was no *you* for him any more, he began to notice me, to be kind, to talk to me about his life and his painting—" She drew a deep breath, and her voice cleared. "That's over—all over. It's as if I couldn't either hate him or love him. There's only the child now—my child. He doesn't even know of it—why should he? It's none of his business; it's nobody's business but mine. But surely you must see I can't give up my baby."

Delia Ralston stood speechless, looking away from her cousin in a growing horror. She had lost all sense of reality, all feeling of safety and self-reliance. Her impulse was to close her ears to the other's appeal as a child buries its head from midnight terrors. At last she drew herself up, and spoke with dry lips.

"But what do you mean to do? Why have you come to me? Why have you told me all this?"

"Because he loved you!" Charlotte Lovell stammered out; and the two women stood and faced each other.

Slowly the tears rose to Delia's eyes and rolled down her cheeks, moistening her lips. Through them she saw her cousin's haggard countenance waver and droop like a drowning face under water. Things half guessed, obscurely felt, surged up from unsuspected depths in her. It was almost as if, for a moment, this other woman were telling her of her own secret past, putting into crude words all the trembling silences of her heart.

The worst of it was, as Charlotte said, that they must act now; there was not a day to lose. Chatty was right—it was impossible that she should marry Joe if to do so meant giving up the child. But in any case, how could she marry him without telling him the truth? And was it conceivable that, after hearing it, he should not repudiate her? All these questions spun agonizingly through Delia's brain, and through them glimmered the persistent vision of the child—Clem Spender's child—growing up on charity, in a negro hovel, or herded in one of the plague-houses they called asylums. No: the child came first—she felt it in every fiber of her body. But what should she do, of whom take counsel, how advise the wretched creature who had come to her in Clement's name? Delia glanced about her desperately, and then turned back to her cousin.

"You must give me time. I must think. You ought not to marry him—and yet all the arrangements are made; and the wedding presents. . . . There would be a scandal. . . . It would kill Granny Lovell. "

Charlotte answered in a low voice: "There *is* no time. I must decide now."

Delia pressed her hands against her breast. "I tell you I must think. I wish you would go home—or, no: stay here—your mother mustn't see your eyes. Jim's not coming home till late; you can wait in this room till I come back." She had opened the wardrobe, and was reaching up for a plain bonnet and heavy veil.

"Stay here? But where are you going?"

"I don't know. I want to walk—to get the air. I think I want to be alone." Feverishly she had unfolded her Paisley shawl, tied on bonnet and veil, thrust her mittened hands into her muff. Charlotte, without moving, stared at her dumbly from the sofa.

"You'll wait?" Delia insisted, on the threshold.

"Yes; I'll wait."

Delia shut the door and hurried down the stairs.

CHAPTER III

SHE HAD spoken the truth in saying that she did not know where she was going. She simply wanted to get away from Charlotte's unbearable face, and from the immediate atmosphere of her tragedy. Out-side, in the open, perhaps it would be easier to think.

As she skirted the park-rails, she saw her rosy children play-ing, under their nurse's eye, with the pampered progeny of other Park-dwellers. The little girl had on her new plaid velvet bonnet and white tippet, and the boy his Highland cap and broadcloth spencer. How happy and jolly they looked! The nurse spied her, but she shook her head, waved at the group and hurried on.

She walked and walked through the familiar streets decked with bright winter sunshine. It was early afternoon, an hour when the gentlemen had just returned to their offices, and there were few pedestrians in Irving Place and Union Square. Delia crossed the Square to Broadway.

The Lovell house in Mercer Street was a sturdy, old-fashioned brick dwelling. A large stable adjoined it, opening on an alley such as Delia, on her honeymoon trip to England, had heard called a "mews." She turned into the alley, entered the stable court, and pushed open a door. In a shabby whitewashed room a dozen children, gathered about a stove, were playing with broken toys. The Irishwoman who had charge of them was cutting out small garments on a broken-legged deal table. She raised a friendly face, recognizing Delia as the lady who had once or twice been to see the children with Miss Charlotte.

★ ★ ★

Delia paused, embarrassed.

"I—I came to ask if you need any new toys," she stammered.

19

"That we do, ma'am. And many another thing too, though Miss Charlotte tells me I'm not to beg of the ladies that comes to see our poor darlin's."

"Oh, you may beg of me, Bridget," Mrs. Ralston answered, smiling. "Let me see your babies—it's so long since I've been here."

The children had stopped playing, and huddled against their nurse, gazed up open-mouthed at the rich, rustling lady. One little girl with pale brown eyes and scarlet cheeks was dressed in a plaid alpaca frock trimmed with imitation coral buttons that Delia remembered. They had been on "best-dress" the year she came out. Delia stooped and took up the child. Its curly hair was brown, the exact color of the eyes—thank heaven! But the eyes had the same little green spangles floating in their transparency. Delia sat down, and the little girl, standing on her knee, gravely fingered her watch-chain.

"Oh, ma'am—maybe her shoes'll soil your skirt. The floor ain't none too clean."

Delia shook her head, and pressed the child against her. She had forgotten the other gazing babies and their wardress. The little creature on her knee was made of different stuff—it had not needed the plaid alpaca and coral buttons to single her out. Her brown curls grew in points on her high forehead, exactly as Clement Spender's did. Delia laid a burning cheek against the forehead.

"Baby want my lovely yellow chain?"

Baby did.

Delia unfastened it and hung it about the child's neck. The other babies clapped and crowed, but the little girl, gravely dimpling, continued to finger the chain in silence.

"Oh, ma'am, you can't leave that fine chain on little Teeny. When she has to go back to those blacks—"

"What is her name?"

"Teena they call her, I believe. It don't seem a Christian name, har'ly."

Delia was silent.

"What I say is, her cheeks is too red. And she coughs too easy. Always one cold and another. Here, Teeny, leave the lady go."

Delia stood up, loosening the tender arms.

"She doesn't want to leave go of you, ma'am. Miss Chatty ain't been in yet, and she's kinder lonesome without her. She don't play like the other children, somehow. . . . Teeny, you look at that lovely chain you've got. . . . There, there now! "

"Good-by, Clementina," Delia whispered below her breath. She kissed the pale brown eyes, the curly crown, and dropped her veil on rushing tears. In the stableyard she dried them on her large embroidered handkerchief, and stood hesitating. Then with a decided step she turned toward home.

The house was as she had left it, except that the children had come in; she heard them romping in the nursery as she went down the passage to her bedroom. Charlotte Lovell was seated on the sofa, upright and rigid, as Delia had left her.

"Chatty—Chatty, I've thought it out. Listen: Whatever happens, the baby sha'n't stay with those people. I mean to keep her."

Charlotte stood up, tall and white. The eyes in her thin face had grown so dark that they seemed like spectral hollows in a skull. She opened her lips to speak; and then, snatching at her handkerchief, pressed it to her mouth and sank down again. A red trickle dripped through the handkerchief onto her poplin skirt.

"Charlotte-Charlotte! " Delia screamed, on her knees beside her cousin. Charlotte's head slid back against the cushions, and the trickle ceased. She closed her eyes, and Delia, seizing a vinaigrette from the dressing-table, held it to her pinched nostrils. The room was filled with an acrid aromatic scent.

Charlotte's lids lifted. "Don't be frightened. I still spit blood sometimes—not often. My lung is nearly healed. But it's the terror—"

"No, no: there's to be no more terror. I tell you I've thought it all out. Jim is going to let me take the baby."

The girl raised herself haggardly. "Jim? Have you told him? Is that where you've been?"

"No, darling. I've only been to see the baby."

"Oh!" Charlotte moaned, leaning back again. Delia took her own handkerchief, and wiped away the tears that were raining down her cousin's cheeks.

"You mustn't cry, Chatty; you must be brave. Your little girl and his—how could you think? But you must give me time: I must manage it in my own way. . . . Only trust me."

Charlotte's lips stirred faintly.

"The tears—don't dry them, Delia. I like to feel them. "

* * *

The two cousins leaned against each other without speaking. The ormolu clock ticked out the measure of their mute communion in minutes, quarters, a half-hour, then an hour: the day declined and darkened; the shadows lengthened across the garlands of the Axminster carpet and the broad white bed. There was a knock.

"The children's waiting to say their grace before supper, ma'am."

"Yes, Eliza. Let them say it to you. I'll come later." As the nurse's steps receded, Charlotte Lovell disengaged herself from Delia's embrace.

"Now I can go," she said.

"You're not too weak, dear? I can send for a coach to take you home."

"No, no; it would frighten Mother. And I shall like walking now, in the darkness. Sometimes the world used to seem all one awful glare to me. There were days when I thought the sun would never set. And then there was the moon at night." She laid her hands on her cousin's shoulders. "Now it's different. By and by I sha'n't hate the light."

The two women kissed each other, and Delia whispered: "Tomorrow."

CHAPTER IV

THE RALSTONS gave up old customs reluctantly; but once they had adopted a new one, they found it impossible to understand why everyone else did not do likewise.

When Delia, who came of the laxer Lovells, and was naturally inclined to novelty, had first proposed to her husband to dine at six o'clock instead of two, his malleable young face had become as relentless as that of the old original Ralston in his grim Colonial portrait. But after a two days' resistance, he had come round to his wife's view, and now smiled contemptuously at the obstinacy of those who clung to a heavy midday meal and high tea.

"There's nothing I hate like narrow-mindedness. Let people eat when they like, for all I care: it's their narrow-mindedness that I can't stand."

Delia was thinking of this as she sat in the drawing-room (her mother would have called it the parlor) waiting for her husband's return. She had just had time to smooth her glossy braids, and slip on the black-and-white striped silk with cherry pipings which was his favorite dress. The drawing-room, with its Nottingham lace curtains looped back under florid gilt cornices, its marble center-table on a carved rosewood foot, and its old-fashioned mahogany armchairs covered with one of the new French silk damasks, in a tart shade of apple-green, was one for any young wife to be proud of. The rosewood whatnots on each side of the folding doors that led into the dining-room were adorned with tropical shells, feldspar vases, an alabaster model of the Leaning Tower of Pisa, a pair of obelisks made of scraps of porphyry and serpentine picked up by the young couple in the Roman Forum, a small bust of Clytie in *biscuit de Sèvres*, and four old-fashioned figures of the Seasons in Chelsea ware, that had to be left among the newer knick-knacks because they had belonged to Great-grandmamma Ralston. On the damask wall-paper hung

23

large dark steel-engravings of Cole's "Voyage of Life," and on the table lay handsomely tooled copies of Turner's "Rivers of France," Drake's "Culprit Fay," Crabbe's "Tales," and "The Book of Beauty," containing portraits of the British peeresses who had participated in the Earl of Eglinton's tournament.

As Delia sat there, before the hard-coal fire in its arched opening of black marble, her citron-wood work-table at her side, and one of the new French lamps shedding a pleasant light on the center-table from under a crystal-fringed shade, she asked herself how she could have passed, in such a short time, so completely out of her usual circle of impressions and convictions—so much farther than ever before beyond the Ralston horizon. Here it was, closing in on her again, as if the very plaster ornaments of the ceiling, the forms of the furniture, the cut of her dress, had been built out of Ralston prejudices, and turned to adamant by the touch of Ralston hands.

She must have been mad, she thought, to have committed herself so far to Charlotte; yet turn about as she would in the ever-tightening circle of the problem, she could still discover no other issue. Somehow, it lay with her to save Clem Spender's baby.

She heard the sound of the latchkey (her heart had never beat so high at it), and the putting down of a tall hat on the hall console—or two tall hats, was it? The drawing-room door opened, and two high-stocked and ample-coated young men came in—two Jim Ralstons, so to speak. Delia had never before noticed how much her husband and his cousin Joe were alike: it made her feel how justified she was in always thinking of the Ralstons collectively.

She would not have been young, and tender, and a happy wife, if she had not thought Joe but an indifferent copy of her Jim; yet allowing for defects in the reproduction, there remained a striking likeness between the two tall, athletic figures, the short, sanguine faces with straight noses, straight whiskers, straight brows, the candid blue eyes and sweet, selfish smiles. Only, at the present moment, Joe looked like Jim with a toothache.

"Look here, my dear: here's a young man who's asked to take potluck with us." Jim smiled, with the confidence of a well nourished husband who knows that he can always bring a friend home unannounced.

"How nice of you, Joe!—Do you suppose he can put up with oyster soup and a stuffed goose?" Delia beamed upon her husband.

"I knew it! I told you so, my dear chap! He said you wouldn't like it—that you'd be fussed about the dinner. Wait till you're married, Joseph Ralston!" Jim brought down a genial paw on his cousin's bottle-green shoulder, and Joe grimaced as if the tooth had stabbed him."

It's excessively kind of you, Cousin Delia, to take me in this evening. The fact is—"

"Dinner first, my boy, if you don't mind! A bottle of Burgundy will brush away the blue devils. Your arm to your cousin, please; I'll just go and see that the wine is brought up."

★　★　★

Oyster soup, broiled shad, stuffed goose, corn fritters and green peppers, followed by one of Grand-mamma Ralston's famous caramel custards: through all her mental anguish, Delia was faintly aware of a secret pride in her achievement. Certainly it would serve to confirm the rumor that Jim Ralston could always bring a friend home to dine without notice. The Ralston and Lovell wines rounded off the effect, and even Joe's drawn face had mellowed by the time the Lovell Madeira started westward. Delia marked the change when the two young men rejoined her in the drawing-room.

"And now, my dear fellow, you'd better tell her the whole story," Jim counseled, pushing an armchair toward his cousin.

The young woman, bent above her wool-work, listened with lowered lids and flushed cheeks. As a married woman—as a mother—Joe hoped she would think him justified in speaking to her frankly: he had her husband's authority to do so.

"Oh, go ahead, go ahead," chafed the exuberant after-dinner Jim from the hearth-rug.

Delia listened, considered, let the bridegroom flounder on through his exposition. Her needle hung like a sword of Damocles above the canvas: she saw at once that Joe depended on her trying to win Charlotte over to his way of thinking. But he was very much in love; at a word from Delia, she understood that he would yield, and Charlotte gain her point, save the child, and marry him.

How easy it was, after all! A friendly welcome, a good dinner, a ripe wine, and the memory of Charlotte's eyes—so much the more expressive for all that they had looked upon. A secret envy stabbed the wife who had lacked this last enlightenment.

How easy it was—and yet it must not be! Whatever happened, she could not let Charlotte Lovell marry Joe Ralston. All the traditions of honor and probity in which she had been brought up forbade her to connive at such a plan. She could conceive—had already conceived—of high-handed measures, swift and adroit defiances of precedent, subtle revolts against the heartlessness of social routine. But a lie she could never connive at. The idea of Charlotte's marrying Joe Ralston—her own Jim's cousin—without revealing her past to him seemed to Delia as dishonorable as it would have seemed to any Ralston. And to tell him the truth would at once put an end to the marriage; of that even Chatty was aware. Social tolerance was not dealt in the same measure to men and to women, and neither Delia nor Charlotte had ever wondered why: like all the young women of their class, they simply bowed to the ineluctable.

No: there was no escape from the dilemma. As clearly as it was Delia's duty to save Clem Spender's child, so clearly, also, she seemed destined to sacrifice his mistress. As the thought pressed on her she remembered Charlotte's wisful cry, "I want to be married, like all of you," and her heart tightened. But yet it must not be.

* * *

"I make every allowance," Joe was droning on, "for my sweet girl's ignorance and inexperience—for her lovely purity. How could a man wish his future wife to be—to be otherwise? You're with me, Jim? And Delia? I've told her, you understand, that she shall always have a special sum for her poor children, in addition to her pin-money—on that she may absolutely count. God! I'm willing to draw up a deed, a settlement, before a lawyer, if she says so. I admire. I appreciate her generosity. But I ask you, Delia, as a mother—mind you, now, I want your frank opinion. If you think I can stretch a point—can let her go on giving her personal care to the children until—until,"—a flush of pride suffused the potential father's brow,—"till nearer duties claim her. . . . Why, I'm more than ready—if you'll tell her so, I undertake." Joe proclaimed, suddenly tingling with the memory of his last glass, "to make it right with my mother, whose prejudices, of course, while I respect them, I can never allow to—to come between me and my own convictions." He sprang to his feet, and beamed on his dauntless double in the chimney-mirror. "My convictions," he flung back at it.

"Hear, hear!" cried Jim emotionally.

Delia's needle gave the canvas a sharp prick, and she pushed her work aside.

"I think I understand you both, Joe. Certainly, in Charlotte's place, I should never give up those children.

"There you are, my dear fellow!" Jim triumphed, as proud of this vicarious courage as of the perfection of dinner.

"Never," said Delia. "Especially, I mean the foundlings—there are two, I think. Those children always if they are sent to asylums. That is what is haunting Chatty."

"Poor innocents! How I love her for loving them! That there should be such scoundrels upon this earth unpunished! Delia, will you tell her that I'll do whatever—"

"Gently, old man, gently," Jim admonished, with a flash of Ralston caution.

"Well, whatever—in reason—"

Delia lifted an arresting hand. "I'll tell her, Joe: she will be grateful. But it's of no use."

"No use? What more—"

"Nothing more—except this. Charlotte has had a return of her old illness. She coughed blood here today. You must not marry her."

There: it was done. She stood up, trembling in every bone, and feeling herself pale to the lips. Had she done right? Had she done wrong? And would she ever know?

Poor Joe turned on her a face as wan as hers: he clutched the back of his armchair, his head drooping forward like an old man's. His lips moved, but made no sound.

"My God!" Jim stammered. "But you know you've got to pull yourself together, old boy."

"I'm—I'm so sorry for you, Joe. She'll tell you tomorrow." Delia faltered, while her husband continued to proffer heavy consolations.

"Take it like a man, old chap. Think of yourself—your future. Can't be, you know. Delia's right—she always *is*. Better get it over—better face the music now than later."

"Now than later," Joe echoed with a tortured grin; and it occurred to Delia that never before in the course of his easy, good-natured life had he had—any more than her Jim—to give up anything his heart was set on. Even the vocabulary of renunciation, and its conventional gestures, were unfamiliar to him.

"But I don't understand. I can't give her up," he declared, blinking away boyish tears.

"Think of the children, my dear fellow; it's your duty," Jim admonished him, checking a glance of pride at Delia's wholesome comeliness.

In the long conversation that followed between the cousins—argument, counter-argument, sage counsel and hopeless protest—

Delia took but an occasional part. She knew enough what the end
would be. The bridegroom who had feared that his bride might
bring home contagion from her visits to the poor would not know-
ingly implant disease in his race. Nor was that all. Too many sad
instances of mothers prematurely fading, and leaving their husbands
alone with a young flock to rear, must be pressing upon Joe's memory. Ralstons, Lovells, Lannings, Archers, Van der Luydens—which
one of them had not some grave to care for in a distant cemetery,
graves of young relatives "in a decline," sent abroad to be cured by
balmy Italy? The Protestant graveyards of Rome and Pisa were full
of New York names; and the vision of that familiar pilgrimage with
a dying wife was one to turn the most ardent Ralston cold. And all
the while, as she listened with bent head, Delia kept repeating to
herself. "This is easy; but how am I to tell Charlotte? "

When poor Joe, late that evening, wrung her hand with a stammered farewell, she called him back abruptly.

"You must let me see her first, please; you must wait till she sends
for you." And she winced a little at the alacrity of his acceptance.
But no amount of rhetorical bolstering-up could make it easy for
a young man to face what lay ahead of Joe; and her final glance at
him was one of compassion.

★   ★   ★

The front door closed upon Joe, and she was roused by her husband's touch on her shoulder.

"I never admired you more, darling. My wise Delia!"

Her head bent back, she took his kiss; and then drew away. The
sparkle in his eyes she understood to be as much an invitation to
her bloom as a tribute to her sagacity.

"What should you have done, Jim, if I'd had to tell you about
myself what I've just told Joe about Chatty?"

A slight frown showed that he thought the question negligible,
and hardly in her usual taste. "Come!" His strong arm entreated her.

She continued to stand away from him, with grave eyes. "Poor
Chatty! Nothing left now—"

His own eyes grew grave in sympathy. At such moments he was
still the sentimental boy whom she could manage.

"Ah, poor Chatty, indeed!" He groped for the readiest panacea.
"Lucky, after all, she has those paupers, isn't it? I suppose a woman
must have children to love—somebody else's, if not her own." It was
evident that the remedy had already relieved his pain.

"Yes," she agreed, "I see no other comfort for her. I'm sure Joe will feel that too. Between us, darling,"—and now she let him have her hands,—"between us, you and I must see to it that she keeps her babies."

"Her babies?" He smiled at the possessive pronoun. "Of course, poor girl! Unless she's sent to Italy?"

"Oh, she won't be that—where's the money to come from? And besides, she'd never leave Aunt Lovell. But I thought, dear, if I might tell her tomorrow,—you see, I'm not exactly looking forward to my talk with her,—if I might tell her that you would let me look after the baby she's most worried about, the poor little foundling girl who has no name and no home,—if I might put aside a fixed sum from my pin-money—"

Their hands glowed together; she lifted her flushing face to his. Manly tears were in his eyes: ah, how he triumphed in her health, her wisdom, her generosity!

"Not a penny from your pin-money!"

She feigned discouragement and wonder. "Think, dear—if I'd had to give you up!"

"Not a penny from your pin-money, I say—but as much more as you need, to help poor Chatty's pauper. There—will that content you?"

"Dearest! When I think of our own upstairs!" They held each other, awed by that evocation.

CHAPTER V

CHARLOTTE LOVELL, at the sound of her cousin's step on the threshold, lifted a fevered face from the pillow. The bedroom, dim and close, smelt of eau de Cologne and fresh linen. Delia, blinking in from the bright winter sun, had to feel her way through a twilight obstructed by dark mahogany.

"I want to see your face, Chatty—unless your head aches too much?"

Charlotte sighed, "No," and Delia drew back the heavy windowcurtains and let a ray of light into the room. In it, she saw the girl's head livid against the bed-linen, the brick-red circles again visible under darkly shadowed lids. Just so poor Cousin So-and-so had looked, the week before she sailed for Italy!

"Delia!" Charlotte breathed.

Delia approached the bed, and stood looking down at her cousin with new eyes. Yes: it had been easy enough, the night before, to dispose of Chatty's future as if it were her own—but now?

"Darling—"

"Oh, begin, please," the girl interrupted, "or I shall know that what's coming is too dreadful!"

"Chatty, dearest, if I promised you too much—"

"Jim won't let you take my child? I knew it! Shall I always go on dreaming things that can never be?"

Delia, her tears running down, knelt by the bed and gave her fresh hand into the other's burning clutch.

"Don't think that, dear; think only of what you'd like best."

"Like best?" The girl rose sharply against her pillows, alive to the hot fingertips.

"You can't marry Joe, dear—can you—and keep little Tina?" Delia continued.

31

"Not keep her with me, no—but somewhere where I could slip off to see her. Oh, I had hoped such follies!"

"Give up follies, Charlotte. Keep her where? See your own child in secret? Always in dread of disgrace? Of wrong to your other children? Have you ever thought of that?"

"Oh, my poor head won't think! You're trying to tell me that I must give her up?"

"No, dear—but that you must not marry Joe."

Charlotte sank back on the pillow, her eyes half-closed. "I tell you I must make my child a home. Delia, you're too blessed to understand!"

"Think yourself blessed too, Chatty. You sha'n't give up your baby. She shall live with you: you shall take care of her—for me."

"For you?"

"I promised you I'd take her, didn't I? But not that you should marry Joe. Only that I would make a home for your baby. Well, that's done: you shall always be together."

Charlotte clung to her and sobbed. "But Joe—I can't tell him, I can't." She put back Delia suddenly. "You haven't told him of my—of my baby? I couldn't bear to hurt him as much as that."

"I told him that you coughed blood yesterday. He'll see you presently: he's dreadfully unhappy. He considers that, in view of your bad health, the engagement is broken by your wish—and he accepts your decision; but if he weakens, or if you weaken, I can do nothing for you or for little Tina. For heaven's sake, remember that."

Delia released her hold, and Charlotte leaned back silent, with closed eyes. On a chair near the bed lay the poplin with red velvet ribbons which had been made over in honor of her betrothal. A pair of new slippers of bronze kid peeped from beneath its folds. Poor Chatty! She had hardly had time to be pretty.

Delia sat by the bed motionless, her eyes on the closed face. They followed the course of two tears that forced a way between Charlotte's tight lids, hung on the lashes, glittered slowly down the cheeks. As the tears reached Chatty's lips, she spoke.

"Shall I live with her somewhere, do you mean? Just she and I?"

"Just you and she."

"In a little house?"

"In a little house."

"You're sure, Delia?"

"Sure, my dearest."

Charlotte once more raised herself on her elbow and slipped a hand under her pillow. She drew out a narrow ribbon on which hung a diamond cluster ring.

"I had taken it off already," she said, and handed it to Delia.

CHAPTER VI

EVERYONE AGREED afterward that you could always have told that Charlotte Lovell was meant to be an old maid. Even before her illness, it had been manifest: there was something prim about her, in spite of her fiery hair. Lucky enough for her, poor girl, considering her wretched health in her youth: Mrs. James Ralston's contemporaries, for instance, remembered Charlotte as a mere ghost, coughing her lungs out—that, of course, had been the reason for breaking her engagement with Joe Ralston.

True, she had recovered very rapidly, in spite of the peculiar treatment she was given. The Lovells, as everyone knew, couldn't afford to send her to Italy; so she was packed off to a farmhouse on the Hudson,—a little place on the James Ralstons' property,—where she lived for five or six years with an Irish servant-woman and a foundling baby. The story of the foundling was another queer episode in Charlotte's history. From the time of her first illness, when she was only twenty-two or -three, she had developed an almost morbid tenderness for children, especially for the children of the poor. It was said—Dr. Lanskell was understood to have said—that the baffled instinct of motherhood was peculiarly intense in cases where lung-disease prevented marriage. And so, when the Doctor decided that Chatty must break her engagement to Jim Ralston and go to live in the country, the Doctor had told her family that the only hope of saving her lay in not separating her entirely from her poor children, but in letting her choose one of them, the youngest and most pitiable, and devote herself to its care. So the James Ralstons had lent her their little farmhouse; and Mrs. Jim, with her extraordinary gift of taking things in at a glance, had at once arranged everything, and even pledged herself to look after the baby if Charlotte died.

35

Charlotte did not die till long afterward. She lived to grow robust and middle-aged, energetic and even tyrannical. And as the transformation in her character took place, she became more and more like the typical old maid: precise, methodical, absorbed in trifles, and attaching an exaggerated importance to the smallest social and domestic observances. Such was her reputation as a vigilant housewife that when poor Jim Ralston was killed by a fall from his horse, and left Delia, still young, with a boy and girl to bring up, it seemed perfectly natural that the heartbroken widow should take her cousin to live with her and share her task.

But Delia Ralston never did things quite like other people. When she took Charlotte, she took Charlotte's foundling too—a little dark-haired girl with pale brown eyes, and the odd, incisive manner of children who have lived too much alone. The little girl was called Tina Lovell: it was vaguely supposed that Charlotte had adopted her. She grew up on terms of affectionate equality with her young Ralston cousins, and almost as much so—it might be said—with the two women who mothered her. But by a natural instinct of imitation which no one thought it necessary to correct, she always called Delia Ralston "Mamma," and Charlotte Lovell "Aunt Chatty." She was a brilliant and engaging creature, and people marveled at poor Chatty's luck in having chosen so interesting a specimen among her foundlings—for she was by this time supposed to have had a whole asylumful to choose from.

The agreeable elderly bachelor, Sillerton Jackson, returning from a prolonged sojourn in Paris (where he was understood to have been made much of by the highest personages), pronounced himself immensely struck with Tina's charms when he saw her at her coming-out ball, and asked Delia's permission to come some evening and dine alone with her and her young people. He complimented the widow on the rosy beauty of her own young Delia; but the mother's keen eye perceived that all the while he was watching Tina, and after dinner he confided to the older ladies that there was something "very French" in the girl's way of doing her hair, and that in the capital of all the elegances she would have been pronounced extremely stylish.

"Oh—" Delia deprecated beamingly, while Charlotte Lovell sat bent over her work with pinched lips; but Tina, who had been laughing with her cousins at the other end of the room, was around upon her elders in a flash.

"I heard what Mr. Sillerton said! Yes, I did, Mamma: he says I do my hair stylishly. Didn't I always tell you so? I *know* it's more becoming to let it curl as it wants to than to plaster it down with bandoline like Aunty's—"

"Tina, Tina—you always think people are admiring you!" Miss Lovell protested.

"Why shouldn't I, when they do?" the girl laughingly challenged; and turning her mocking eyes on Sillerton Jackson: "Do tell Aunt Charlotte not to be so dreadfully old-maidish!"

Delia saw the blood rise to Charlotte Lovell's face. It no longer painted two brick-rose circles on her thin cheek-bones, but diffused a harsh flush over her whole countenance, from the collar fastened with an old-fashioned garnet brooch to the pepper-and-salt hair (with no trace of red left in it) flattened down over her hollow temples.

That evening, when they went up to bed, Delia called Tina into her room. "You ought not to speak to your Aunt Charlotte as you did just now, dear. It's disrespectful—and it hurts her."

The girl overflowed with compunction. "Oh, I'm so sorry! Because I said she was an old maid? But she *is*, isn't she, Mamma? In her inmost soul, I mean. I don't believe she's ever been young— ever thought of fun or admiration or falling in love—do you? That's why she never understands me, and you always do, you darling dear Mamma." With one of her light movements Tina was in the widow's arms.

"Child, child!" Delia softly scolded, kissing the dark curls planted in five points on the girl's forehead.

★ ★ ★

There was a footfall in the passage, and Charlotte Lovell stood in the doorway. Delia, without moving, gave her a glance of welcome over Tina's shoulder.

"Come in, Charlotte. I'm scolding this child for behaving like a spoilt baby before Sillerton Jackson. What will he think of her?"

"Just what she deserves, probably," Charlotte returned with a cold smile. Tina went toward her, and she kissed the girl's proffered forehead just where Delia's warm lips had touched it. "Good night, child," she said, in her dry tone of dismissal.

The door closed on the two women, and Delia signed to Charlotte to take the armchair opposite her own.

"Not so near the fire," Miss Lovell answered. She chose a straight-backed chair, and sat down with folded hands. Delia's eyes rested absently on the thin, ringless hands: she wondered why Charlotte never wore her mother's jewels.

"I heard what you were saying to Tina, Delia. You were scolding her because she called me an old maid."

It was Delia's turn to color. "I scolded her for being disrespectful, dear; if you heard what I said, you can't think that I was too severe."

"Not too severe: no. I've never thought you too severe with Tina: on the contrary."

"You think I spoil her?"

"Sometimes."

Delia felt an unreasoning resentment. "What was it I said that you object to?"

Charlotte returned her glance steadily. "I would rather she thought me an old maid than—"

"Oh—" Delia murmured. With one of her quick leaps of intuition, she had entered into the other's soul, and measured its shuddering loneliness.

"What else," Charlotte inexorably pursued, "*can* she possibly be allowed to think me—ever?"

"I see—I see—" the widow faltered.

"A ridiculous, narrow-minded old maid—nothing else," Charlotte Lovell insisted, getting to her feet, "or I shall never feel safe with her."

"Good night, my dear," Delia said compassionately. There were moments when she almost hated Charlotte for being Tina's mother, and others, such as this, when her heart was wrung by the tragic spectacle of that unavowed bond.

Charlotte seemed to have divined her thought.

"Oh, but don't pity me! She's mine," she murmured, going.

CHAPTER VII

DELIA RALSTON sometimes felt that the real events of her life did not begin until both her children had contracted—ever so safely and suitably—the usual irreproachable New York alliances. The boy had married first, choosing a Vandergrave in whose father's bank at Albany he was to have an immediate junior partnership; and young Delia (as her mother had foreseen she would) had selected John Junius, the safest and soundest of the many young Halseys, and followed him to his parents' house the year after her brother's marriage.

After young Delia left the house in Gramercy Park, it was inevitable that Tina should take the center front of its narrow stage. Tina had reached the marriageable age; she was admired and sought after; but what hope was there of her finding a husband? The two watchful women did not propound this question to each other; but Delia Ralston, brooding over it day by day, and taking it up with her when she mounted at night to her old-fashioned bedroom, knew that Charlotte Lovell, at the same hour, carried the same problem with her to the floor above.

The two cousins, during their eight years of life together, had seldom openly disagreed. Indeed, it might almost have been said that there was nothing open in their relation. Delia would have had it otherwise: after they had once looked so deeply into each other's souls, it seemed unnatural that a veil should fall between them. But she understood that Tina's ignorance of her origin must at all costs be preserved, and that Charlotte Lovell, abrupt, passionate and inarticulate, knew of no other security than to wall herself up in perpetual silence.

So far had she carried this self-imposed reticence that Mrs. Ralston was surprised at her suddenly asking, soon after young Delia's marriage, to be allowed to move down into the small bedroom next to Tina's, left vacant by the bride's departure.

"But you'll be so much less comfortable there, Chatty. Have you thought of that? Or is it on account of the stairs?"

"No; it's not the stairs," Charlotte answered with her usual bluntness. How could she avail herself of the pretext Delia offered her, when Delia knew that she still ran up and down the three flights like a girl? "It's because I should be next to Tina," she said, in a low voice that jarred like an untuned string.

"Oh—very well. As you please." Mrs. Ralston could not tell why she felt suddenly irritated by the request, unless it were that she had already amused herself with the idea of fitting up the vacant room as a sitting-room for Tina. She had meant to do it in pink and pale green, like an opening flower.

"Of course, if there is any reason—" Charlotte suggested, as if reading her thought.

"None whatever, except that—well, I'd meant to surprise Tina by doing the room up as a sort of little boudoir, where she could have her books and things, and see her girl friends."

"You're too kind, Delia; but Tina mustn't have boudoirs." Miss Lovell answered ironically, the green specks showing in her eyes.

"Very well: as you please," Delia repeated in the same irritated tone. "I'll have your things brought down tomorrow."

Charlotte paused in the doorway. "You're sure there's no other reason?"

"Other reason? Why should there be?" The two women looked at each other almost with hostility, and Charlotte turned to go.

The talk once over, Delia was annoyed with herself for having yielded to Charlotte's wish. Why must it always be she who gave in, she who, after all, was the mistress of the house, and to whom both Charlotte and Tina might almost be said to owe their very existence, or at least all that made it worth having? Yet whenever any question arose about the girl, it was invariably Charlotte who gained her point, Delia who yielded: it was as if Charlotte, in her mute, obstinate way, were determined to take every advantage of the dependence that made it impossible for a woman of Delia's nature to oppose her.

In truth, Delia had looked forward more than she knew to the quiet talks with Tina to which the little boudoir would have lent itself. While her own daughter inhabited the room, Mrs. Ralston had been in the habit of spending an hour there every evening, chatting with the two girls while they undressed, and listening to their comments on the incidents of the day. She always knew beforehand exactly what her own girl would say; but Tina's views and opinions were a perpetual delicious shock to her. Not that they were unfamiliar: there were moments when they seemed to well straight up from the dumb depths of her own past. Only they expressed feelings that she had never uttered, ideas she had hardly avowed to herself: Tina sometimes said things which Delia Ralston, in far-off self-communions, had imagined herself saying to Clem Spender.

And now there would be an end to these evening talks: if Charlotte had asked to be lodged next to her daughter, might it not conceivably be because she wished them to end? It had never before occurred to Delia that her influence over Tina might be resented; now it flashed a light far down into the abyss which had always divided the two women. But a moment later Delia reproached herself for attributing feelings of jealousy to her cousin. Was it not rather to herself that she should have ascribed them? Charlotte, as Tina's mother, had every right to wish to be near her, near her in all senses of the word: what claim had Delia to oppose to that natural privilege? Next morning she ordered Charlotte's things taken down to the room next to Tina's.

That evening, when bedtime came, Charlotte and Tina went up stairs together; but Delia lingered in the drawing-room on the pretext of having letters to write. In truth, she dreaded to pass the threshold where, evening after evening, the fresh laughter of the two girls had waylaid her, while Charlotte Lovell already slept her old-maid sleep on the floor above. It sent a pang through Delia to think that henceforth she would be cut off from this means of keeping her hold on Tina.

An hour later, when she mounted the stairs in her turn, she was guiltily conscious of moving as noiselessly as she could along the heavy carpet of the corridor, and of pausing longer than was necessary over the extinguishing of the gas-jet on the landing. As she stood there she strained her ears for the sound of voices from the doors behind which Charlotte and Tina slept; she would have been secretly hurt at hearing talk and laughter from within. But none came to her; nor was there any light beneath the doors. Evidently Charlotte, in her hard, methodical way, had said good night to her daughter on reaching her room, and gone straight to bed as usual. Perhaps she had never approved of Tina's vigils, of the long undressing punctuated with mirth and confidences; it was not unlikely, Delia reflected, that she had asked to have the room next to her daughter's simply because she wished the girl not to miss her "beauty sleep."

Whenever Delia tried to explore the secret of her cousin's actions, she returned from the adventure humiliated and abashed by the base motives she attributed to Charlotte. How was it that she, Delia Ralston, whose happiness had been open and avowed to the world, so often found herself denying poor Charlotte the secret of her scanted motherhood? She hated herself for this moment of envy whenever she detected it; and tried to atone for it by a softened manner and a more anxious consideration for Charlotte's feelings; but the attempt was not always successful, and Delia sometimes wondered if Charlotte did not resent any too open show of sympathy as an indirect glance at her misfortune. The worst of suffering such as hers was that it left one sore to the gentlest touch.

Delia, slowly undressing before the same lace-draped toilet-glass which had reflected her bridal image, was turning over these thoughts when she heard a faint knock on her door. On the threshold stood Tina in a dressing-gown, her dark curls falling over her shoulders. With a happy heartbeat Delia held out her arms.

"I had to say good night, Mamma," the girl whispered.

"Of course, dear." Delia kissed her lifted forehead. "But run off now, or you might disturb your aunt. You know she sleeps badly, and you must be as quiet as a mouse now she's next to you."

"Yes, I know," Tina acquiesced, with a grave glance that was almost of complicity.

She asked no further question; she did not linger; lifting Delia's hand, she held it a moment against her cheek, and then stole out as noiselessly as she had come.

CHAPTER VIII

"BUT YOU must see," Charlotte Lovell insisted, laying aside the Evening *Post*, "that Tina has changed. You do see that?"

The two women were sitting alone by the drawing-room fire in Gramercy Park. Tina had gone to dine with her cousin, Delia Halsey, and was to be taken afterward to a ball at the Vandergraves', from which the John Juniuses had promised to see her home. Mrs. Ralston and Charlotte, their early dinner finished, had the long evening to themselves. It was their custom, on such occasions, for Charlotte to read the news aloud to her cousin, while the latter embroidered; but tonight, all through Charlotte's conscientious progress from column to column, without a slip or an omission, Delia had felt her, for some special reason, alert to take advantage of her daughter's absence.

To gain time, Mrs. Ralston bent over a dropped stitch in her delicate white embroidery.

"Tina changed? Since when?" she questioned.

The answer flashed out instantly. "Since Lanning Halsey has been coming here so much."

"Lanning? I used to think he came for Delia," Mrs. Ralston mused, speaking at random to gain still more time.

"It's natural you should suppose that everyone came for Delia," Charlotte rejoined dryly; "but as Lanning continues to seek every chance of being with Tina—"

* * *

Mrs. Ralston stole a swift glance at her cousin. She had in truth noticed that Tina had changed, as a flower changes at the mysterious moment when the unopened petals flush from within. The girl had grown handsomer, shyer, more silent, at times more irrelevantly gay. But Delia had not associated these variations of mood with the presence of Lanning Halsey, one of the numerous youths who had haunted the house before young Delia's marriage. There had, indeed, been a moment when Mrs. Ralston's eyes had been fixed, with a certain apprehension, on the handsome Lanning. Among all the sturdy and stolid Halsey cousins he was the only one to whom a prudent mother might have hesitated to intrust her daughter: it would have been hard to say why, except that he was handsomer and more talkative than the rest, chronically unpunctual, and totally unperturbed by the fact. Clem Spender had been like that; and what if young Delia—?

But young Delia's mother was speedily reassured. The girl, herself arch and appetizing, took no interest in the corresponding graces except when backed by more solid qualities. A Ralston to the core, she demanded the Ralston virtues, and chose the Halsey most worthy of a Ralston bride.

Mrs. Ralston felt that Charlotte was waiting for her to speak. "It will be hard to get used to the idea of Tina's marrying," she said gently. "I don't know what we two old women shall do, alone in this empty house—for it will be an empty house then. But I suppose we ought to face the idea."

"I *do* face it," said Charlotte Lovell gravely.

"And you dislike Lanning? I mean as a husband for Tina?"

Miss Lovell folded the evening paper and stretched out a thin hand for her knitting. She glanced across the citron-wood work-table at her cousin. "Tina must not be too difficult—" she began.

"Oh—" Delia protested, reddening.

"Let us call things by their names," the other evenly pursued. "That's my way, when I speak at all. Usually, as you know, I say nothing."

The widow made a sign of assent and Charlotte went on: "It's better so. But I've always known a time would come when we should have to talk things out."

"Talk things out? You and I? What things?"

"Tina's future."

There was a silence. Delia Ralston, who always responded instantly to the least appeal to her sincerity, breathed a deep sigh of relief. At last the ice in Charlotte's breast was breaking up!

"My dear," Delia murmured, "you know how much Tina's hap-piness concerns me. If you disapprove of Lanning Halsey as a husband, have you any other candidate in mind?"

Miss Lovell smiled one of her faint hard smiles. "I am not aware that there is a queue at the door. Nor do I disapprove of Lanning Halsey as a husband. Personally, I find him very agreeable: I understand his attraction for Tina."

"Ah—Tina *is* attracted?"

"Yes."

Mrs. Ralston pushed aside her work and thoughtfully considered her cousin's sharply lined face. Never had Charlotte Lovell more completely presented the typical image of the old maid than as she sat there, upright on her straight-backed chair, with narrowed elbows and clicking needles, and imperturbably discussed her daughter's marriage.

"I don't understand, Chatty. Whatever Lanning's faults are,—and I don't believe they're grave,—I share your liking for him. After all,"—Mrs. Ralston paused,—"what is it that people find so reprehensible in him? Chiefly, as far as I can hear, that he can't decide on the choice of a profession. The New York view about that is rather narrow, as we know. Young men may have other tastes—artistic—literary; they may even have difficulty in deciding."

Both women colored slightly, and Delia guessed that the same reminiscence which shook her own bosom also throbbed under Charlotte's straitened bodice.

Charlotte spoke. "Yes: I understand that. But hesitancy about a profession may cause hesitancy about—other decisions."

"What do you mean? Surely not that Lanning—?"

"Lanning has not asked Tina to marry him."

"And you think he's hesitating?"

* * *

Charlotte paused. The steady click of her needles punctuated the silence as once, years before, it had been punctuated by the tick of the Parisian clock on Delia's mantel. As Delia's memory fled back to that scene, she felt its mysterious tension in the air.

Charlotte spoke. "Lanning is not hesitating any longer: he has decided not to marry Tina. But he has also decided—not to give up seeing her."

Delia flushed abruptly: she was irritated and bewildered by Charlotte's oracular phrases, doled out between parsimonious lips.

"You don't mean that he has offered himself and then drawn back? I can't think him capable of such an insult to Tina."

"He has not insulted Tina. He has simply told her that he can't afford to marry. Until he chooses a profession, his father will allow him only a few hundred dollars a year; and that may be suppressed, if—if he marries against his parents' wishes."

It was Delia's turn to be silent. The past was too overwhelmingly resuscitated in Charlotte's words. Clement Spender stood before her, irresolute, impecunious, persuasive. Ah, if only she had let herself be persuaded!

"I'm very sorry that this should have happened to Tina. But as Lanning appears to have behaved honorably, and withdrawn without raising false expectations, we must hope—we must hope—" Delia paused, not knowing what they must hope.

Charlotte Lovell laid down her knitting. "You know as well as I do, Delia, that every young man who is attracted by Tina will find as good reasons for not marrying her."

"Then you think his withdrawal a pretext?"

"Naturally. The first of many that will be found by his successors—for of course he will have successors. Tina—attracts."

"Ah," Delia murmured.

Here they were at last face to face with the problem which, through all the years of silence and evasiveness, had lain as close to the surface as a body too hastily concealed! Delia drew another deep breath, which again was almost one of relief. She had always known that it would be difficult, almost impossible, to find a husband for Tina; and much as she desired Tina's happiness, some inmost selfishness whispered how much less lonely and purposeless the close of her own life would be should the girl be forced to share it. But how say this to Tina's mother?

"I hope you exaggerate, Charlotte. There may be disinterested characters. But in any case, surely Tina need not be unhappy here, with us who love her so dearly."

"Tina an old maid? Never!" Charlotte Lovell rose abruptly, her closed hand crashing down on the slender work-table. "My child shall have her life,—her own life,—whatever it costs me."

Delia's ready sympathy welled up. "I understand your feeling. I should want also—hard as it will be to let her go. But surely there is no hurry—no reason for looking so far ahead. The child is not twenty. Wait."

Charlotte stood before her, motionless, perpendicular. At such moments she made Delia think of lava struggling through granite: there seemed no issue for the fires within.

"Wait? But if *she* doesn't wait?"

"But if he has withdrawn—what do you mean?"

"He has given up marrying her—but not seeing her."

Delia sprang up in her turn, flushed and trembling.

"Charlotte! Do you know what you are insinuating?"

"Yes: I know."

"But it's too outrageous. No decent girl—"

The words died on Delia's lips. Charlotte Lovell held her eyes inexorably. "Girls are not always what you call decent," she declared.

Mrs. Ralston turned slowly back to her seat. Her tambour frame had fallen to the floor: she stooped heavily to pick it up. Charlotte hung over her, relentless as doom.

"I can't imagine, Charlotte, what is gained by saying such things—even by hinting them. Surely you trust your own child—"

Charlotte laughed. "My mother trusted me," she said.

"How dare you—how dare you?" Delia began; but her eyes fell, and she felt a tremor of weakness in her throat.

"Oh, I dare anything for Tina, even to judging her as she is," Tina's mother murmured.

"As she is? She's perfect."

"Let us say, then, that she must pay for my imperfections. All I want is that she shouldn't pay too heavily."

Mrs. Ralston sat silent. It seemed to her that Charlotte spoke with the voice of all the dark destinies coiled under the safe surface of life; and that to such a voice there was no answer but an awed acquiescence.

"Poor Tina!" she breathed.

"Oh, I don't mean that she shall suffer! It's not for that that I've waited—waited. Only I've made mistakes: mistakes that I understand now, and must remedy. You've been too good to us—and we must go."

"Go?" Delia gasped.

"Yes. Don't think me ungrateful. You saved my child once—do you suppose I can forget? But now it's my turn—it's I who must save her. And it's only by taking her away from everything here from everything she's known till now—that I can do it. She's lived too long among unrealities: and she's like me. They won't content her!"

"Unrealities?" Delia echoed vaguely.

"Unrealities for her. Young men who make love to her and can't marry her. Happy households where she's welcomed till she's suspected of designs on a brother or a husband—or else exposed to their insults. How could we ever have imagined, either of us, that the child could escape disaster? I thought only of her present happiness—of all the advantages, for both of us, of being with you. But this affair with young Halsey has opened my eyes. I must take Tina away. We must go and live somewhere where we're not known, where we shall be among plain people, leading plain lives. Somewhere where she can find a husband, and make herself a home."

Charlotte paused. She had spoken in a rapid, monotonous tone, as if by rote; but now her voice broke, and she repeated painfully: "I'm not ungrateful."

"Oh, don't let's speak of gratitude! What place has it between you and me?"

* * *

Delia had risen and begun to move uneasily about the room. She longed to plead with Charlotte, to implore her not to be in haste, to picture to her the cruelty of severing Tina from all her habits and associations, of carrying her inexplicably away to lead "a plain life among plain people." What chance was there, indeed, that a creature so radiant could tamely submit to such a fate, or find an acceptable husband in such conditions? The change might only precipitate a tragedy. Delia's experience was too limited for her to picture exactly what might happen to a girl like Tina, suddenly cut off from all that sweetened life for her; but vague visions of revolt and flight—of a "fall" deeper and more irretrievable than Charlotte's—flashed through her agonized imagination.

"It's too cruel—it's too cruel," she cried, speaking to herself rather than to Charlotte.

Charlotte, instead of answering, glanced abruptly at the clock.

"Do you know what time it is? Past midnight! I mustn't keep you sitting up for my foolish girl."

Delia's heart contracted. She saw that Charlotte wished to cut the conversation short, and to do so by reminding her that only Tina's mother had a right to decide what Tina's future should be. At that moment, though Delia had just protested that there could be no question of gratitude between them, Charlotte Lovell seemed to her a monster of ingratitude, and it was on the tip of her tongue to cry out: "Have all the years then given me no share in Tina?" But at the same instant she had put herself once more in Charlotte's place, and was feeling the mother's fierce terrors for her child. It was natural enough that Charlotte should resent the faintest attempt to usurp in private the authority she could never assert in public. With a pang of compassion Delia realized that she was literally the one being on earth before whom Charlotte could act the mother. "Poor thing—ah, let her!" she murmured inwardly.

"But why should you sit up for Tina? She has the key, and Delia is to bring her home."

Charlotte Lovell did not immediately answer. She rolled up her knitting, looked severely at one of the candelabra on the mantelpiece, and crossed over to straighten it. Then she picked up her work-bag.

"Yes, as you say—why should anyone sit up for her?" She moved about the room, blowing out the lamps, covering the fire, assuring herself that the windows were bolted, while Delia passively watched her. Then the cousins lighted their candles and walked upstairs through the darkened house. Charlotte seemed determined to make no further allusion to the subject of their talk. On the landing she paused, bending her head toward Delia's nightly kiss.

"I hope they've kept up your fire," she said, with her capable housekeeping air; and on Delia's hasty reassurance, the two murmured a simultaneous "Good night," and Charlotte turned down the passage to her room.

CHAPTER IX

DELIA'S FIRE had been kept up, and her dressing-gown was warming on an armchair near the hearth. But she neither undressed nor yet seated herself. Her conversation with Charlotte had filled her with a deep unrest.

For a few moments she stood in the middle of the floor, looking slowly about her. Nothing had ever been changed in the room which, even as a bride, she had planned to modernize. All her dreams of renovation had faded long ago. Some deep central indifference had gradually made her regard herself as a third person, living the life meant for another woman, a woman totally unrelated to the vivid Delia Lovell who had entered that house so full of plans and visions. The fault, she knew, was not her husband's. With a little managing and a little wheedling, she would have gained every point as easily as she had gained the capital one of taking the foundling baby under her wing. The difficulty was that, after that victory, nothing else seemed worth trying for. The first sight of little Tina had somehow decentralized Delia Ralston's whole life, making her indifferent to everything else, except indeed the welfare of her own husband and children. Ahead of her she saw only a future full of duties, and these she had gayly and faithfully accomplished. But her own life was over: she felt as detached as a cloistered nun.

The change in her was too deep not to be visible. The Ralstons openly gloried in dear Delia's conformity. Each acquiescence passed for a concession, and their doctrine was fortified by such fresh proofs of its durability. Now, as Delia glanced about her at the Leopold Robert lithographs, the family daguerreotypes, the rosewood and mahogany, she understood that she was looking at the walls of her own grave.

The change had come on the day when Charlotte Lovell, cower-ing on that very lounge, had made her terrible avowal.

51

Then for the first time Delia, with a kind of fearful, exaltation, had heard the blind forces of life groping and crying underfoot. But that day also she had known herself excluded from them, doomed to dwell among shadows. Life had passed her by, and left her with the Ralstons.

Very well, then! She would make the best of herself, and of the Ralstons. The vow was immediate and unflinching; and for nearly twenty years she had gone on observing it. Once only had she been, not a Ralston but herself; once only had it seemed worth while. And now perhaps the same challenge had sounded again; again, for a moment, it might be worth while to live. Not for the sake of Clement Spender—poor Clement, married years ago to a plain determined cousin, who had hunted him down in Rome, and inclosing him in an unrelenting domesticity, had obliged all New York on the grand tour to buy his pictures with a resigned grimace. No, not for Clement Spender, hardly for Charlotte or Tina, but for her own sake, hers, Delia Ralston's, for the sake of her one missed vision, her forfeited reality, she would once more break down the Ralston barriers and reach out into the world.

A faint sound through the silent house disturbed Delia Ralston's meditation. Listening, she heard Charlotte Lovell's door open, and her stiff petticoats rustle toward the landing. A light glanced under the door and vanished; Charlotte had passed the threshold on her way downstairs.

Without moving, Delia continued to listen. Perhaps the careful Charlotte had gone down to make sure that the front door was not bolted, or that she had really covered up the fire. In that case, her step would presently be heard returning. But no step sounded; and it became gradually evident that Charlotte had gone downstairs to wait for her daughter. Why?

Delia's room was at the front of the house. She stole across the heavy carpet, drew aside the curtains and cautiously folded back the inner shutters. Below her lay the empty square, white with moonlight, its tree-trunks patterned on a fresh sprinkling of snow. The houses opposite slept in darkness: not a footstep broke the white surface; not a wheel-track marked the brilliant street. Overhead a heaven full of stars swam in the moonlight.

★   ★   ★

Of the households around Gramercy Park Delia knew that only two others had gone to the ball: the Petrus Vandergraves and their cousins, the young Parmly Ralstons. The Lucius Lannings had just entered on their three years of mourning for Mrs. Lucius' mother (it was hard on their daughter Kate, just eighteen, who would be unable to "come out" till she was twenty-one); young Mrs. Marcy Mingott was "expecting her third," and consequently secluded from the public eye for nearly a year; and the other denizens of the Square belonged to the undifferentiated and uninvited.

Delia pressed her forehead against the pane. Before long, carriages would turn the corner, and the sleeping square ring with hoof-beats; fresh laughter and young farewells would mount from the doorsteps. But why was Charlotte waiting for her daughter downstairs in the darkness?

The Parisian clock struck one. Delia came back into the room, raked the fire, picked up a shawl, and wrapped in it, returned to her vigil. Ah, how old she must have grown, that she should feel the cold at such a moment! It reminded her of what the future held for her: neuralgia, rheumatism, stiffness, accumulating infirmities. And never had she kept a moonlight watch with a lover's arms to warm her.

The square still lay silent. Yet the ball must surely be ending: the gayest dances did not last long after one in the morning, and the drive from University Place to Gramercy Park was a short one. Delia leaned in the embrasure and listened.

Hoof-beats sounded in Irving Place, and the Petrus Vandergraves' family coach drew up before the opposite house. The Vandergrave girls and their brother sprang out and mounted the steps; then the coach stopped a few doors farther on, and the Parmly Ralstons, brought home by their cousins, descended at their own door. The next carriage that rounded the corner must therefore be the John Juniuses, bringing Tina.

* * *

The gilt clock struck half-past one. Delia wondered, knowing that young Delia, out of regard for John Junius' business hours, never stayed late at evening parties. Doubtless Tina had delayed her; Mrs. Ralston felt a little annoyed with Tina's thoughtlessness in keeping her cousin up. But the feeling was swept away by an immediate wave of sympathy. "We must go away somewhere, and lead plain lives among plain people." If Charlotte carried out her threat,—and Delia knew she would hardly have spoken unless her resolve had been taken.—it might be that at that very moment Tina was dancing her last *valse*.

Another quarter of an hour passed; then, just as the cold was penetrating Delia's shawl, she saw two people turn into the deserted square from Irving Place. One was a young man in beaver hat and ample cloak. To his arm clung a feminine figure so closely wrapped and muffled that, until the corner light fell on it, Delia hesitated. After that, she wondered that she had not at once recognized Tina's dancing step, and her manner of tilting her head a little sideways to look up at the person she was talking to.

Tina—Tina and Lanning Halsey, walking home alone in the small hours from the Vandergrave ball! Delia's first thought was of an accident: the carriage might have broken down, or her daughter been taken ill and obliged to return home. But no: in the latter case she would have sent the carriage on with Tina. And if there had been an accident of any sort, the young people would have been hastening to apprise Mrs. Ralston; instead of which, through the bitter brilliant night, they sauntered like lovers in a midsummer glade, and Tina's thin slippers might have been treading daisies instead of snow.

Delia began to tremble like a girl. In a flash she had the answer to a question which had long been the subject of her secret conjectures. How did lovers like Charlotte and Clement Spender contrive to meet? What Latmian solitude hid their clandestine joys? In the exposed, compact little society to which they all belonged, how was it possible, literally—for such things to happen? Delia would never have dared to put the question to Charlotte; there were moments when she almost preferred not to know, not even to hazard a guess. But now, at a glance, she understood. How often Charlotte Lovell, staying alone in town with her infirm grandmother, must have walked home from evening parties with Clement Spender, how often have let herself and him into the darkened house in Mercer Street, where there was no one to spy upon their coming but a deaf old lady and her aged servants, all securely sleeping overhead. Delia, at the thought, saw the grim drawing-room which had been their moonlit forest, the drawing-room into which old Mrs. Lovell no longer descended, with its swathed chandelier and hard Empire sofas, and the blank-faced caryatids of the mantel; she pictured the shaft of moonlight falling across the swans and garlands of the pompous carpet, and in that icy light two young figures in each other's arms.

* * *

Yes. It must have been some such memory that had roused Charlotte's suspicions, excited her fears, sent her down in the darkness to confront the culprits. Delia shivered at the irony of the confrontation. If Tina had but known! But to Tina, of course, Charlotte was still what she had long since resolved to be: the image of prudish spinsterhood. And Delia could imagine how quietly and decently the scene below stairs would presently be enacted: no astonishment, no reproaches, no insinuations, but a smiling and resolute ignoring of excuses.

"What, Tina? You walked home with Lanning? You imprudent child—in this wet snow! Ah, I see: Delia was worried about the baby, and ran off early, promising to send back the carriage—and it never came? Well, my dear, I congratulate you on finding Lanning to see you home. . . . Yes—I sat up because I couldn't for the life of me remember whether you'd taken the latchkey—was there ever such a flighty old aunt? But don't tell your mamma, dear, or she'd scold me for being so forgetful, and for staying downstairs in the cold. . . . You're quite sure you have the key? Ah, Lanning has it? Thank you, Lanning—so kind. Good night—or one really ought to say, good morning!"

As Delia reached this point in her mute representation of Charlotte's monologue, the front door slammed below, and young Lanning Halsey walked slowly away across the square. Delia saw him pause on the opposite pavement, look up at the unlit house-front, and then turn lingeringly away. His dismissal had taken exactly as long as Delia had calculated it would. A moment later she saw a passing light under her door, heard the starched rustle of Charlotte's petticoats, and knew that mother and daughter had reached their rooms.

Slowly, with stiff motions, she began to undress, blew out her candles, and knelt long by her bedside, her face hidden.

CHAPTER X

LYING AWAKE till morning, Delia lived over every detail of the fateful day when she had assumed the charge of Charlotte's child. At the time she had been hardly more than a child herself, and then there had been no one for her to turn to, no one to fortify her resolution, or to advise her how to put it into effect. Since then, the accumulated experiences of seventeen years ought to have prepared her for emergencies, and taught her to advise others instead of seeking their guidance. But these years of experience weighed on her like chains binding her down to her narrow plot of life: independent action struck her as more dangerous, less conceivable, than when she had first ventured on it. There seemed to be so many more people to "consider" now ("consider" was the Ralston word): her children, their children, the families into which they had married. What would the Halseys say, and what the Ralstons? Had she then become a Ralston through and through?!

A few hours later she sat in old Dr. Lanskell's library, her eyes on his sooty Smyrna rug. Dr. Lanskell no longer practiced: at most, he went to a few old patients, gave consultations in "difficult" cases. But he remained a power in his own kingdom, a sort of lay pope or medical elder, to whom the patients he had healed of physical ills now returned for moral medicine. People were agreed that Dr. Lanskell's judgment was sound; but what secretly drew them to him was the fact that, in the most totem-ridden of communities, he was known not to be afraid of anything.

Now, as Delia sat by his grate, and watched his massive silver-headed figure moving ponderously about the room, between rows of calf bindings, and the Dying Gladiators and Young Augustuses of grateful patients, she already felt the reassurance communicated by his mere bodily presence.

"You see, when I first took Tina, I didn't perhaps consider sufficiently—"

The Doctor halted behind his desk and brought his fist down on it in a genial thump. "Thank God you didn't! There are considerers enough in this town without you, Delia Lovell. "

She looked up quickly. "Why do you call me Delia Lovell?"

"Well, because today I rather suspect you *are*," he rejoined astutely; and she met this with a wistful laugh.

"Perhaps, if I hadn't been, once before—I mean, if I'd always been a prudent deliberate Ralston, it would have been kinder to Tina in the end."

Dr. Lanskell sank his gouty bulk into the chair behind his desk, and beamed at her through ironic spectacles. "I hate in-the-end kindnesses: they're about as nourishing as the third day of cold mutton."

She pondered. "Of course, I realize that if I adopt Tina—"

"Yes?"

"Well, people will say—" A deep blush rose to her throat, covered her cheeks and brow, and ran like fire under her decently parted hair.

He nodded: "Yes."

"Or else"—the blush darkened—"that she's Jim's—"

Again Dr. Lanskell nodded. "That's what they're more likely to think; and what's the harm if they do? I know Jim: he asked no questions when you took the child—but he knew whose she was."

She raised astonished eyes. "He knew?"

"Yes: he came to me. And—well—in the baby's interest, I violated professional secrecy. That's how Tina got a home. You're not going to denounce me, are you?"

"Oh, Dr. Lanskell!" Her eyes filled with painful tears. "Jim knew? And didn't tell me?"

"No. People didn't tell each other things much in those days, did they? But he admired you enormously for what you did. And if you assume—as I suppose you do—that he's now in a world of com-pleter enlightenment, why not take it for granted that he'll admire you still more for what you're going to do? Presumably," the Doctor concluded sardonically, "people realize in heaven that it's a devilish sight harder, on earth, to do a brave thing at fifty than at twenty-five."

"Ah, that's what I was thinking this morning," she confessed.

"Well, you're going to prove the contrary this afternoon." He looked at his watch, stood up and laid a fatherly hand on her shoulder. "Let people think what they choose; and send young Delia to me if she gives you any trouble. Your boy wont, you know, nor John Junius either; it must have been a woman who invented that third and-fourth-generation idea."

An elderly maidservant looked in, and Delia rose; but on the threshold she halted. "I have an idea it's Charlotte I may have to send to you."

"Charlotte?"

"She'll hate what I'm going to do, you know."

Dr. Lanskell lifted his silver eyebrows, "Yes: poor Charlotte! I suppose she's jealous? That's where the truth of the third-and fourth-generation business comes in, after all. Somebody always has to foot the bill."

"Ah—if only Tina doesn't!"

"Well—that's just what Charlotte will come to recognize. So your course is clear."

He guided her out through the brown dining-room, where some poor people and one or two old patients were already waiting.

* * *

Delia's course, in truth, seemed clear enough till, that afternoon, she summoned Charlotte alone to her bedroom. Tina was lying down with a headache: it was the accepted attitude of young ladies in sentimental dilemmas, and greatly simplified the communion of their elders.

Delia and Charlotte had exchanged only conventional phrases over their midday meal; but Delia had the sense that her cousin's resolution was definitely taken. The events of the previous evening had evidently confirmed Charlotte's view that the time had come for decisive measures.

Miss Lovell, closing the bedroom door with her dry deliberate-ness, advanced toward the chintz lounge between the windows.

"You wanted to see me, Delia?"

"Yes.—Oh, don't sit there," Mrs. Ralston exclaimed uncontrollably.

* * *

Charlotte stared: was it possible that she did not remember the sobs of anguish she had once smothered in those cushions?

"Not—"

"No; came nearer. Sometimes I think I'm a little deaf," Delia nervously explained, pushing a chair up to' her awn.

"Ah!" Charlotte seated herself. "I hadn't remarked it. But if you are, it may have saved you from hearing at what hour of the morning Tina came back from the Vandergraves. She would never for-give herself—inconsiderate as she is—if she thought she'd waked you."

"She didn't wake me," Delia answered. Inwardly she thought: "Charlotte's mind is made up; I sha'n't be able to move her."

"I suppose Tina enjoyed herself very much at the ball?" she continued.

"Well, she's paying for it with a sick headache. Such excitements are not meant for her. I've already told you—"

"Yes," Mrs. Ralston interrupted. "It's to continue our talk that I've asked you to come up this afternoon. "

"To continue it?" The brick-red circles appeared in Charlotte's dried cheeks. "Is it worth while? I think I ought to tell you at once that my mind's made up. You must recognize that I know what's best for Tina."

"Yes; of course. But wont you at least allow me a share in your decision?"

"A share?"

Delia leaned forward, laying a warm hand on her cousin's inter-locked fingers. "Charlotte, once in this room you asked me to help you—you believed I could. Wont you believe it again?"

Charlotte's lips grew rigid. "I believe the time has come for me to help myself."

"At the cost of Tina's happiness?"

"No; but to spare her greater unhappiness."

"But Charlotte. Tina's happiness is all I want."

"Oh, I know. You've done all you could do for my child."

"No, not all." Delia rose, and stood before her cousin with a kind of solemnity. "But now I'm going to." It was as if she had pronounced a vow.

Charlotte looked up with a glitter of apprehension in her eyes.

"If you mean that you're going to use your influence with the Halseys—I'm very grateful to you; I shall always be grateful. But I don't want a compulsory marriage for my child."

Delia flushed at the other's incomprehension. It seemed to her that her purpose must be written on her face. "I'm going to adopt Tina—give her my name," she said.

Charlotte stared at her stonily. "Adopt her—adopt her?"

"Don't you see, dear, the difference it will make? There's my mother's money—the Lovell money; it is not much, to be sure;

but Jim always wanted it to go back to my family. And my Delia and her brother are so handsomely provided for. There's no reason why my little fortune shouldn't go to Tina—and why she shouldn't be known as Tina Ralston." Delia paused. "I believe—I think I know—that Jim would have approved of that too. "

"*Approved?*"

"Yes. Can't you see that when he let me take the child, he must have foreseen and accepted whatever—might come of it?"

Charlotte stood up also. "Thank you, Delia. But nothing more must come of it, except our leaving you—our leaving you now. I'm sure that's what Jim would have approved."

Mrs. Ralston drew back a step or two. Charlotte's cold resolution benumbed her courage, and she could find no immediate reply.

"Ah, then it's easier for you to sacrifice Tina's happiness than your pride?"

"My pride? I've no right to any pride, except in my child. And that I'll never sacrifice."

"No one asks you to. You're not reasonable. You're cruel. All I want is to be allowed to help Tina, and you speak as if I were interfering with your rights."

"My rights?" Charlotte caught her up again. "What are they? I have no rights, either before the law or in the heart of my own child."

"How can you say such things? You know how Tina loves you."

"Yes—compassionately, as I used to love my old-maid aunts. There were two of them—you remember? Like withered babies! We children used to be warned never to say anything that might shock Aunt Josie or Aunt Nonie, exactly as I heard you telling Tina the other night—"

"Oh—" Delia murmured.

Charlotte Lovell stood before her, haggard, rigid, unrelenting. "No, it's gone on long enough. I mean to tell her everything—and to take her away."

"To tell her about her birth? "

"I was never ashamed of it," Charlotte panted.

"You sacrifice her, then—sacrifice her to your desire for mastery?"

The two women faced each other, both with weapons spent. Delia, through the tremor of her own indignation, saw her antagonist slowly waver, step backward, sink down with a broken murmur on the lounge. Charlotte hid her face in the cushions, clenching them with violent hands. The same fierce maternal passion that had once flung her down upon those same cushions was now bowing her still lower, in the throes of a bitterer renunciation. Delia seemed to hear again the old cry: "But how can I give up my baby?" Her own momentary resentment melted, and she bent over the mother's laboring shoulders.

"Chatty—it won't be like giving her up this time. Can't we just go on loving her together?"

Charlotte did not answer. For a long time she lay silent, immovable, her face hidden: she seemed to fear to turn it to the face bent down to her. But presently Delia was aware of a gradual relaxing of the stretched muscles, and saw that one of her cousin's hands was stirring and groping. She lowered her hand to the seeking fingers, and it was caught and pressed to Charlotte's lips.

CHAPTER XI

TINA LOVELL—now Miss Clementina Ralston—was to be married in July to Lanning Halsey. The engagement had been announced only in the previous April; and the female elders of the tribe had begun by crying out against the indelicacy of so' brief a betrothal. It was unanimously agreed in New York that "young people should be given the time to get to know each other;" and though the greater number of the couples constituting New York society had played together as children, and been born of parents as long and as familiarly acquainted, yet some mysterious law of decorum required that the newly affianced should always be regarded as being also newly acquainted. In the Southern States things were differently conducted: headlong engagements, even runaway marriages, were not uncommon in the annals of Virginia and Maryland; but such rashness was less consonant with the sluggish blood of New York, where the pace of life was still set with a Dutch deliberateness.

In a case as unusual as Tina Ralston's, however, it was hardly surprising that tradition had been disregarded. In the first place, everyone knew that she was no more Tina Ralston than you or I—unless, indeed, one were to credit the rumors about poor Jim's unsuspected "past," and his widow's magnanimity. But the opinion of the majority was against this. People were reluctant to charge a dead man with an offense from which he could not clear himself; and the Ralstons unanimously declared that, thoroughly as they disapproved of Mrs. James Ralston's action, they were convinced that she would not have adopted Tina had her doing so appeared to "cast a slur" on her late husband's morals.

No: the girl was perhaps a Lovell,—though even that idea was not generally held,—but she was certainly not a Ralston. Her black eyes and flighty ways too obviously excluded her from the clan for any formal excommunication to be pronounced against her. In fact, most people believed that—as Dr. Lanskell had always affirmed—her origin was really undiscoverable, that she represented one of the unsolved mysteries which occasionally perplex and irritate well regulated societies, and that her adoption by Delia Ralston was simply one more proof of the Lovell clannishness, since the child had been taken in by Mrs. Ralston only because her cousin Charlotte was so attached to it. To say that Mrs. Ralston's son and daughter were pleased with the idea of Tina's adoption would have been an exaggeration; but they abstained from comment, minimizing the effect of their mother's whim by a dignified silence. It was the old New York way for families thus to screen the eccentricities of an individual member, and where there was "money enough to go around," the heirs would have been thought vulgarly grasping to protest at the alienation of a small sum from the general inheritance.

Nevertheless, Delia Ralston, from the moment of Tina's adoption, was perfectly aware of a different attitude on the part of her children. They dealt with her patiently, almost paternally, as with a minor in whom one juvenile lapse has been condoned, but who must be subjected, in consequence, to a stricter vigilance; and society treated her in the same indulgent but guarded manner.

She had (it was Sillerton Jackson who first phrased it) an undoubted way of "carrying things off;" since Mrs. Manson Mingott had broken her husband's will, nothing like it had been seen in New York. But Mrs. Ralston's method was different, and less easy to analyze. What Mrs. Manson Mingott had accomplished with epigram, invective, insistency and runnings to and fro, the other achieved without raising her voice or seeming to take a step from the beaten path. When she had persuaded Jim Ralston to take in the foundling baby, it had been done in the turn of a hand, one didn't know when or how; and the next day he and she were as untroubled and beaming as usual. And now, this adoption! Well, she had pursued the same method; as Sillerton Jackson said, she behaved as if her adopting Tina had always been an understood thing, as if she wondered that people should wonder. And in face of her wonder, theirs seemed foolish, and they gradually desisted.

In reality, behind Delia's assurance there was a tumult of doubts and uncertainties. But she had once learned that one can do almost anything (perhaps even murder) if one does not attempt to explain it; and the lesson had never been forgotten. She had never explained the taking over of the foundling baby; nor was she now going to explain its adoption. She was just going about her business as if nothing had happened that needed to be accounted for; and a long inheritance of moral modesty helped her to keep her questionings to herself.

These questionings were in fact less concerned with public opinion than with Charlotte Lovell's private thoughts. Charlotte, after her first moment of tragic resistance, had shown herself pathetically, almost painfully, grateful. That she had reason to be, Tina's attitude abundantly revealed. Tina, during the first days after her return from the Vandergrave ball, had shown a closed and darkened face that terribly reminded Delia of the ghastliness of Charlotte Lovell's sudden reflection, years before, in her own bedroom mirror. The first chapter of the mother's history was already written in the daughter's eyes; and the Spender blood in Tina might well precipitate the sequence. In those few hours of silent observation Delia perceived, with terror and compassion, the justification of Charlotte's misgivings. The girl had nearly been lost to them both: at all costs such a risk must not be renewed.

The Halseys, on the whole, had behaved, admirably. Lanning wished to marry dear Delia Ralston's protégée—was shortly, it was understood, to take her adopted mother's name, and inherit her fortune. To what more could a Halsey aspire than one more alliance with a Ralston? The families had always intermarried. The Halsey parents gave their blessing with a precipitation which made it evident that they too had their anxieties, and that the relief of seeing Lanning "settled" would more than compensate for the conceivable drawbacks of the marriage—though, once it was decided on, they would not admit such drawbacks existed. For old New York always thought away whatever interfered with the perfect propriety of its arrangements.

Charlotte Lovell of course perceived and recognized all this. She accepted the situation—in her private hours with Delia—as one more in the long list of mercies bestowed on an undeserving sinner. And one phrase of hers perhaps gave the clue to her acceptance: "Now at least she'll never suspect the truth." It had come to be the poor creature's ruling purpose that her child should never guess the tie between them.

But Delia's chief support was the sight of Tina. The older woman, whose whole life had been shaped and colored by the faint reflection of a rejected happiness, hung dazzled in the light of bliss accepted. Sometimes, as she watched Tina's changing face, she felt as though her own blood were beating in it, as though she could read every thought and emotion feeding those tumultuous currents. Tina's love was a stormy affair, with endless ups and downs of rapture and depression, arrogance and self-abasement; Delia saw displayed before her, with an artless frankness, all the visions, cravings and imaginings of her own stifled youth.

What the girl really thought of her adoption it was not easy to discover. She had been given, at fourteen, the current version of her origin, and had accepted it as carelessly as a happy child accepts some remote and inconceivable fact that does not alter the familiar order of things. And she accepted her adoption in the same spirit. She knew that the name of Ralston had been given to her to facilitate her marriage with Lanning Halsey; and Delia had the impression that all irrelevant questionings were submerged in an overwhelming gratitude. "I've always thought of you as my mamma; and now, you dearest, you really are," she had whispered, her cheek against Delia's; and Delia had laughed back: "Well, if the lawyers, can make me so!" But there the matter dropped, swept away on the current of Tina's bliss. They were all, in those days—Delia, Char-lotte, even the gallant Lanning—rather like straws whirling about on a sunlit torrent.

The golden flood swept them onward, nearer and nearer to the enchanted date; and Delia, deep in bridal preparations, wondered at the comparative indifference with which she had ordered and inspected her own daughter's twelve-dozen-of-everything. There had been nothing to quicken the pulse in young Delia's placid bridal; but as Tina's wedding-day approached, imagination bourgeoned like the year. The wedding was to be celebrated at Lovell Place, the old house on the Sound where Delia Lovell had herself been married, and where, since her mother's death, she spent her summers. Although the neighborhood was already overspread with a network of mean streets, the old house, with its thin colonnaded veranda, still looked across an uncurtailed lawn and leafy shrubberies to the narrows of Hell Gate; and the drawing-rooms kept their frail, slender settees, their Sheraton consoles and cabinets. It had been thought useless to discard them for more fashionable furniture, since the growth of the city made it certain that the place must eventually be sold.

Tina, like Mrs. Ralston, was to have a "house-wedding," though Episcopalian society was beginning to disapprove of such ceremonies, which were regarded as the despised *pis aller* of Baptists, Methodists, Unitarians and the other altarless sects. In Tina's case, however, both Delia and Charlotte felt that the greater privacy of a marriage in the house made up for its more secular character; and the Halseys discreetly favored their decision. The ladies accordingly settled themselves at Lovell Place before the end of June, and every morning young Lanning Halsey's cat-boat was seen beating across the bay, and furling its sail at the anchorage below the lawn.

* * *

There had never been a fairer June in anyone's memory. The damask roses and mignonette below the veranda had never sent such a breath of summer through the tall French windows; the gnarled orange-trees brought out from the old arcaded orange-house had never been so thickly blossomed; the very haycocks on the lawn gave out whiffs of Araby.

The day before the wedding Delia Ralston sat on the veranda watching the moon rise across the Sound. She was tired with the multitude of last preparations, and sad at the thought of Tina's going. On the following evening the house would be empty; till death came, she and Charlotte would sit alone together beside the evening lamp. Such repinings were foolish—they were, she reminded herself, "not like her." But too many memories stirred and murmured in her: her heart was haunted. As she closed the door on the silent drawing-room,—already transformed into a chapel, with its lace-hung altar, the tall alabaster vases awaiting their white roses and June lilies, the strip of red carpet dividing the rows of chairs from door to chancel,—she felt that it had been a mistake to come back to Lovell Place for the wedding. She saw herself again, in her high-waisted "India mull" embroidered with daisies, her satin sandals, her Brussels veil—saw again her reflection in the sallow pier-glass, as she had entered that same room on Jim Ralston's triumphant arm, and the one terrified glance she had exchanged with her own image before she took her stand under the bell of white roses, and smiled upon the congratulating company. Ah, what a different image the pier-glass would reflect tomorrow!

Charlotte Lovell's brisk step sounded in the hall, and she came out and joined Mrs. Ralston.

"I've been to the kitchen to tell Melissa Grimes that she'd better count on two hundred plates of ice-cream."

"Two hundred? Yes—I suppose she had, with all the Philadelphia connection coming." Delia pondered. "How about the doylies?" she inquired.

"With your aunt Cecilia Vandergrave's we shall manage beautifully."

"Yes. . . . Thank you, Charlotte, for taking all this trouble."

"Oh—" Charlotte protested, with her flitting sneer; and Delia perceived the irony of thanking a mother for occupying herself with the details of her own daughter's wedding.

"Do sit down, Chatty," she murmured, feeling herself redden at her blunder.

★ ★ ★

Charlotte, with a sigh, sat down on the nearest chair.

"We shall have a beautiful day tomorrow," she said, pensively surveying the placid heaven.

"Yes. Where is Tina? "

"She was very tired. I've sent her upstairs to lie down."

This seemed so eminently suitable that Delia made no immediate answer. After an interval she said: "We shall miss her."

Charlotte's reply was an inarticulate murmur.

The two cousins remained silent, Charlotte as usual bolt upright, her thin hands clutched on the arms of her old-fashioned rush-bottomed seat, Delia somewhat heavily sunk into the depths of a high-backed armchair. The two had exchanged their last remarks on the preparations for the morrow, and nothing more remained to be said as to the number of guests, the brewing of the punch, the arrangements for the robing of the clergy, and the disposal of the presents in the best spare-room.

★ ★ ★

Only one subject had not yet been touched on, and Delia, as she watched her cousin's profile grimly cut upon the melting twilight, waited for Charlotte to speak. But Charlotte remained silent.

"I have been thinking," Delia at length began, a slight tremor in her voice, "that I ought presently—" She fancied she saw Charlotte's hands tighten on the knobs of the chair-arms.

"You ought presently—? "

"Well, before Tina goes to bed, perhaps go up for a few minutes—" Charlotte remained silent, visibly resolved on making no effort to assist her.

"Tomorrow," Delia continued, "we shall be in such a rush from the earliest moment that I don't see how, in the midst of all the in-terruptions and excitement, I can possibly—"

"Possibly?" Charlotte monotonously echoed.

Delia felt her blush deepening through the dusk. "Well, I suppose you agree with me that a word ought to be said to the child as to the new duties and responsibilities that—well—what is usual, in fact, at such a time," she falteringly ended.

"Yes, I have thought of that," Charlotte answered abruptly. She said no more, but Delia divined in her the stirring of that obscure opposition which, in the crucial moments of Tina's life, seemed automatically to manifest itself. She could not understand why Char-lotte should at times grow so enigmatic and inaccessible, but she saw no reason why this change of mood should interfere with what she deemed to be her own duty. Tina must long for her guiding hand into the new life as much as she yearned for the exchanges of half-confidences which would be her real farewell to her adopted daughter. Her heart beating a little more quickly than usual, she rose and walked through the open window into the shadowy drawing-room. The moon, between the columns of the veranda, sent a broad light across the rows of chairs, irradiated the lacedecked altar with its empty candlesticks and vases, and outlined with silver Delia's heavy reflection in the pier-glass.

* * *

She crossed the room toward the hall.

"Delia!" Charlotte's voice sounded behind her. She turned, and the two women faced each other in the revealing light. Charlotte's face looked as it had looked on the dreadful day when Delia had suddenly seen it in the glass above her shoulder.

"You were going up now—to speak to Tina?" Charlotte asked.

"I—yes. It's nearly nine. I thought—"

"Yes; I understand." Miss Lovell made a visible effort at self-control. "Please understand me too, Delia, if I ask you—not to."

"Not to?" Delia scrutinized her cousin with a vague sense of apprehension. What mystery did this strange request conceal? But no—such a doubt as flitted across her mind was inadmissible. She was too sure of her Tina!

"I confess I don't understand you, Charlotte. You surely feel that, on the night before her wedding, a girl ought to have a mother's counsel, a mother's—"

"Yes: I feel that." Charlotte Lovell took a hurried breath. "But the question is: which of us is her mother?"

Delia drew back involuntarily. "Which of us?" she stammered.

"Yes. Oh, don't imagine it's the first time I've asked myself the question! There—I mean to be calm, quite calm. I don't intend to go back to the past. I've accepted—accepted everything—Grate-fully. Only tonight—just tonight."

Delia felt the rush of pity that always prevailed over every other feeling in her rare interchanges of truth with Charlotte Lovell. Her throat filled with tears, and she remained silent.

"Just tonight," Charlotte concluded, "*I'm* her mother."

"Charlotte! You're not going to tell her so—not now?" broke involuntarily from Delia.

Charlotte gave a faint laugh. "If I did, should you hate it as much as all that?"

"Hate it? What a word, between us!"

"Between us? But it's been between us since the beginning—the very beginning! Since the day when you discovered that Clement Spender hadn't quite broken his heart because he wasn't good enough for you, since you found your revenge and your triumph in keeping me at your mercy and in taking his child from me!" Charlotte's words flamed up as if from the depth of the infernal fires; then the blaze dropped, her head sank forward, and she stood before Delia dumb and stricken.

Delia's first movement was one of an indignant recoil. Where she had felt only tenderness, compassion, the impulse to help and befriend, these darknesses had been smoldering in the other's breast! It was as if a poisonous smoke had swept over some pure summer landscape.

* * *

Usually such feelings were quickly followed by a reaction of sym-pathy. But now she felt none. An utter weariness possessed her.

"Yes," she said slowly, "I sometimes believe you really have hated me from the very first, hated me for everything I've tried to do for you."

Charlotte raised her head sharply. "To do for me? But everything you've done has been done for Clement Spender!"

Delia stared at her with a kind of terror. "You are horrible, Char-lotte. Upon my honor, I haven't thought of Clement Spender for years."

"Ah, but you have—you have! You've always thought of him in thinking of Tina—of him and nobody else! A woman never stops thinking of the man she loves. She thinks of him years afterward, in all sorts of unconscious ways, in thinking of all sorts of things—books, pictures, sunsets, a flower or a ribbon—or a clock on the mantelpiece." Charlotte broke off with her sneering laugh. "That was what I gambled on, you see—that's why I came to you that day. I knew I was giving Tina another mother."

Again the poisonous smoke seemed to envelope Delia: that she and Charlotte, two spent old women, should be standing before Tina's bridal altar and talking to each other of hatred, seemed unimaginably hideous and degrading.

"You wicked woman—you *are* wicked!" she exclaimed.

Then the evil mist cleared away, and through it she saw the baffled pitiful figure of the mother who was not a mother, and who, for every benefit accepted, felt herself robbed of a privilege. She moved nearer to Charlotte and laid a hand on her arm.

"Not here! Don't let us talk like this here."

The other drew away from her. "Wherever you please, then. I'm not particular!"

"But tonight, Charlotte—the night before Tina's wedding? Isn't every place in this house full of her? How could we go on saying cruel things to each other anywhere?" Charlotte was silent, and Delia continued in a steadier voice: "Nothing you say can really hurt me—for long; and I don't want to hurt you—I never did."

"You tell me that—and you've left nothing undone to divide me from my daughter! Do you suppose it's been easy, all these years, to hear her call you mother? Oh, I know, I know—it was agreed that she must never guess. But if you hadn't perpetually come between us, she'd have had no one but me, she'd have felt about me as a child feels about its mother, she'd have had to love me better than anyone else. With all your forbearances and your generosities, you've ended by robbing me of my child. And I've put up with it all for her sake—because I knew I had to. But tonight—tonight she belongs to me. Tonight I can't bear that she should call you mother."

Delia Ralston made no immediate reply. It seemed to her that for the first time she had sounded the deepest depths of maternal passion, and she stood awed at the echoes it gave back.

"How you must love her—to say such things to me!" she murmured; and then, with a final effort: "Yes, you're right. I won't go up to her. It's you who must go."

Charlotte started toward her impulsively; but with a hand lifted as if in defense, Delia moved across the room and out again to the veranda. As she sank down in her chair, she heard the drawing room door open and close, and the sound of Charlotte's feet on the stairs.

* * *

Delia sat alone in the night. The last drop of her magnanimity had been spent, and she tried to avert her shuddering mind from Charlotte. What was happening at this moment upstairs? With what dark revelations were Tina's bridal dreams to be defaced? Well, that was not matter for conjecture, either. She, Delia Ralston, had played her part, done her utmost: there remained nothing now but to try to lift her spirit above the embittering sense of failure.

There was a strange element of truth in some of the things that Charlotte had said. With what divination that maternal passion had endowed her! Her jealousy seemed to have a million feelers. Yes; it was true that the sweetness and peace of Tina's bridal eve had been filled, for Delia, with visions of her own unrealized past. Softly, imperceptibly, it had reconciled her to the memory of what she had missed. All these last days she had been living the girl's life, she had been Tina, and Tina had been her own girlish self, the far-off Delia Lovell. Now, for the first time, without shame, without self-reproach, without a pang or a scruple, Delia could yield to that vision of requited love from which her imagination had always turned away. She had made her choice in youth, and she had accepted it in maturity; and here in this bridal joy, so mysteriously her own, was the compensation for all she had missed and yet never renounced.

Delia understood now that Charlotte had guessed all this, and that the knowledge had filled her with a fierce resentment. Charlotte had said long ago that Clement Spender had never really belonged to her; now she had perceived that it was the same with Clement Spender's child. As the truth stole upon Delia, her heart melted with the old compassion for Charlotte. She saw that it was a terrible, a sacrilegious thing, to interfere with another's destiny, to lay the tenderest touch upon any human being's right to love and suffer after his own fashion. Delia had twice intervened in Charlotte Lovell's life: it was natural that Charlotte should be her enemy. If only she did not revenge herself by wounding Tina!

The adopted mother's thoughts reverted painfully to the little white room upstairs. She had meant her half-hour with Tina to leave the girl with thoughts as fragrant as the flowers she was to find beside her when she woke. And now—

Delia started up from her musing. There was a step on the stair— Charlotte coming down through the silent house. Delia stood up with a vague impulse of escape: she felt that she could not face her cousin's eyes. She turned the corner of the veranda, hoping to find the shutters of the dining-room unlatched, and to slip away unnoticed to her room; but in a moment Charlotte was beside her.

"Delia!"

"Ah, it's you? I was going up to bed." For the life of her Delia could not keep an edge of hardness from her voice.

"Yes: it's late. You must be very tired." Charlotte paused: her own voice was strained and painful.

"I am tired," Delia acknowledged.

In the moonlit hush the other went up to her, laying a timid touch on her arm.

"Not till you've seen Tina."

Delia stiffened. "Tina? But it's late! Isn't she sleeping? I thought you'd stay with her until—"

"I don't know if she's sleeping." Charlotte paused. "I haven't been in—but there's a light under her door."

"You haven't been in?"

"No: I just stood in the passage, and tried—"

" Tried—?"

"To think of something—something to say to her without without her guessing." A sob stopped her, but she pressed on with a final effort. "It's no use. You were right: there's nothing I can say. You're her real mother. Go to her. It's not your fault—or mine."

"Oh—" Delia cried.

Charlotte clung to her in inarticulate abasement. "You said I was wicked—I'm not wicked. After all, she was mine when she was little!"

Delia put an arm about her shoulder.

"Hush, dear! We'll go to her together."

The other yielded automatically to her touch, and side by side the two women mounted the stairs, Charlotte timing her impetuous step to Delia's stiffened movements. They walked down the passage to Tina's door; but there Charlotte Lovell paused and shook her head.

"No—you," she whispered suddenly, and turned away.

⋆   ⋆   ⋆

Tina lay in bed, her arms folded under her head, her happy eyes reflecting the silver space of sky that filled the window. She smiled at Delia through her dream.

"I knew you'd come."

Delia sat down beside her, and their clasped hands lay upon the coverlet. They did not say much, after all; or else their communion had no need of words. Delia never knew how long she sat by the child's side: she abandoned herself to the spell of the moonlit hour.

But suddenly she thought of Charlotte, alone behind the shut door of her own room, watching, struggling, listening. Delia must not, for her own pleasure, prolong that tragic vigil. She bent down to kiss Tina good night then she paused on the threshold and turned back.

"Darling! Just one thing more."

"Yes?" Tina murmured.

"I want you to promise me——"

"Everything, everything, you darling!"

"Well, then, that when you go away tomorrow—at the very last moment, you understand——"

"Yes?"

"After you've said good-by to me, and to everybody else—just as Lanning helps you into the carriage——"

"Yes?"

"That you'll give your last kiss to Aunt Charlotte. Don't forget—the very last."